Analise came to as a heavy weight lifted from her chest.

A scream died on her lips as the shadowy figure looming over her turned into a familiar one.

"Pierce!"

"I thought you were dead," he said, and then she was in his arms, tears she'd fought for so long running freely down her face.

He held on to her as though she was a mirage and he was afraid if he let go she'd disappear.

And then he was leaning back and she knew he was trying to see her through the dim light and she knew it didn't matter if they were blurs to each other. In the next instant, he'd pulled her back against him and, cupping her face in his hands, kissed her lips.

His face was rough with stubble and cold from the snow and it felt wonderful against her skin. He felt real, and his kiss was the fabric of fantasy. Happiness welled inside her like an untamed artisanal well, tickling her from the inside out with the delirious feeling of safety she'd thought she'd never again experience.

ALICE SHARPE

WESTIN'S WYOMING

TORONTO NEW YORK LONDON
AMSTERDAM PARIS SYDNEY HAMBURG
STOCKHOLM ATHENS TOKYO MILAN MADRID
PRAGUE WARSAW BUDAPEST AUCKLAND

This book is dedicated to my daughter-in-law,
Becky Braun, with much love.

Recycling programs
for this product may
not exist in your area.

ISBN-13: 978-0-373-74625-5

WESTIN'S WYOMING

www.Harlequin.com

Printed in U.S.A.

ABOUT THE AUTHOR

Alice Sharpe met her husband-to-be on a cold, foggy beach in Northern California. One year later they were married. Their union has survived the rearing of two children, a handful of earthquakes registering over 6.5, numerous cats and a few special dogs, the latest of which is a yellow Lab named Annie Rose. Alice and her husband now live in a small rural town in Oregon, where she devotes the majority of her time to pursuing her second love, writing.

Alice loves to hear from readers. You can write her at P.O. Box 755, Brownsville, OR 97327. SASE for reply is appreciated.

Books by Alice Sharpe

HARLEQUIN INTRIGUE
746—FOR THE SAKE OF THEIR BABY
823—UNDERCOVER BABIES
923—MY SISTER, MYSELF*
929—DUPLICATE DAUGHTER*
1022—ROYAL HEIR
1051—AVENGING ANGEL
1076—THE LAWMAN'S SECRET SON**
1082—BODYGUARD FATHER**
1124—MULTIPLES MYSTERY
1166—AGENT DADDY
1190—A BABY BETWEEN THEM
1209—THE BABY'S BODYGUARD
1304—WESTIN'S WYOMING‡‡

*Dead Ringer
**Skye Brother Babies
‡‡Open Sky Ranch

CAST OF CHARACTERS

Pierce Westin—When he left the Open Sky Ranch, Pierce was a troublemaker who'd had a falling-out with his father. Fifteen years have gone by and he's back to mind the homestead for a while and maybe mend more than one kind of fence.

Princess Analise Elsbeth Emille—Raised in the small monarchy of Chatioux, this engaged to be married beauty never questioned her destiny—until now.

General Kaare—The king's closest advisor and protocol expert, this old soldier is determined to monitor the princess's behavior and safety whether she likes it or not.

Brad Harley—The princess's new bodyguard, hired after an attack on the original. Is he part of the solution or part of the problem?

Mr. Vaughn—Traveling with the princess, is he more than the meek little man he seems?

Bierta Gulden—The mousy maid seems content to stay in the princess's shadow, but that won't protect her from a killer….

Lucas Garvey—This ranch hand is sworn in to act as a backup bodyguard.

Darrell Cox—Another ranch hand who signs on to help protect Princess Analise—and soon regrets it.

Cody Westin—Pierce's brother who calls him home to fill in for him. He leaves in such a mysterious hurry that no one on the ranch even knows visitors are expected.

Birch Westin—Pierce and Cody's father.

Toby (aka Tex)—A little boy who gets a whole lot more Wild West than he ever bargained for.

Jamie Dirk—Two generations of Westin ranchers have depended on Jamie's knowledge and common sense, but never more than now.

Prologue

February

Cody Westin gripped the receiver in his left hand as he sat down at his desk.

"Tell me exactly where you found her," he said, pausing to listen as the detective rattled off rapid-fire details.

"Yes, I'll come," Cody said at length, his dark gaze moving to the big window that overlooked the uncompromising Wyoming peaks. He glanced at the clock on the wall. "I'll leave within the hour. I'll meet you there." Brow furrowing, he added, "Smyth? Don't lose her, okay?"

He clicked off the phone and stood for a moment. Then he walked to the sideboard and poured himself a finger of whiskey, tossing it back in one swallow, closing his eyes as the liquor burned its way down his throat.

His brother Adam, who worked the ranch with Cody and their father, was off on a backcountry hike in Hawaii, unreachable by phone. That meant Cody would need to contact his other brother, Pierce. The detective's call couldn't have come at a worse time—the ranch was gearing up for calving season, which was coming in a month or so.

"Family comes first," he muttered. It was an uneasy point in ranching life. The herd came first, too. Made things a juggling act.

Pierce was half owner of a business currently operating overseas. He could take time off for an emergency if he wanted to. That was the rub. Would he want to?

He had to. Someone had to be in charge since their father was laid up. The place couldn't run itself.

Clicking nails on the hardwood floor and a wet nose thrust against his arm announced Bonnie had come into the office. Cody ran a hand along the pale yellow Lab's smooth head, then set the empty glass on the sideboard. Back at the desk he didn't even bother to review his planner— whatever was on the books for the next few days would just have to happen without him. He had to go. This might be his last chance.

He moved aside the painting of the old hunting lodge that hung behind the desk and worked the combination on the safe hidden under it. Reaching inside, his fingers closed on a small box. He stared at it a moment, then slowly tucked it in his jeans pocket as the dog watched him with deep brown eyes, tail gently wagging.

"You can't go with me, Bonnie," he murmured. "Not this time."

He would pack a bag, drive to Woodwind and catch a plane. Somehow, someway, he had to find the right words, say the right thing, end this nightmare.

But first he'd call Pierce home.

Chapter One

Pierce Westin stared down at the cattle gate for a long time. Was his brain frozen, were aching muscles clouding his vision or had someone cut the chain and wrapped it back around the steel railings to make it appear it was still secure?

He swung himself off his horse, waded through the snow that had backed up against the gate and grabbed the metal with gloved hands. The last links on either end dangled loose when shaken. It had been cut, all right.

Well, maybe the winter policy had changed since he'd lived and worked on the ranch. Maybe it was always kept this way now. He'd only been back a few days—how did he know?

Except the cuts looked new. He studied the snow, both on his side of the gate and on the Bureau of Land Management side where the ranch had grazing rights. He couldn't see any fresh tracks besides his own.

His horse, a tidy pinto named Sam, bumped

Pierce's hat off his head and whinnied softly against his neck, his exhalations forming a cloud of vapor in the cold air. Pierce caught the hat before it hit the ground and pulled it back on. Okay, okay, no time to worry about this now, he had a chopper to meet and Sam was apparently on duty to remind him of it. Back in the saddle, Pierce moved off down the canyon.

He'd been away from the ranch for most of fifteen years, hence the protesting muscles in the saddle. He wouldn't be here now except for Cody's call, and for a second he flashed on the situation he'd left behind in Italy. He immediately pushed aside those concerns—no use stewing about something he couldn't change from thousands of miles away.

An hour later, Pierce reached the airfield in time to witness a huge helicopter descending from the turbulent skies—there was a storm predicted for late the next day. No point in muttering curses at Cody for leaving nothing but cryptic notes about who was arriving on the chopper, but man, it would have been nice to have a name or a reason for the visit. Even a contact number so he could cancel would have been nice.

The blades were still whirling when Pierce pulled his horse to a halt beside Jamie Dirk. Two generations of Westin men had depended on Jamie's common sense and work ethic to keep the Open Sky running, but the old guy hadn't changed much in the past fifteen years.

Jamie stood beside his bay mare. Pierce knew the preferred mode of transportation had shifted from horseback to ATVs over the years. He was riding the pinto for old time's sake. He suspected Jamie was riding the mare because that was what a ranch hand was "supposed" to ride and there was little doubt that a horse was better with a cow than a machine or even a man if it came to that.

Jamie looked up at Pierce from beneath the brim of his disreputable brown hat, shifted the ever-present toothpick from one side of his mouth to the other and grumbled, "'Bout time you showed up."

"You know anything about the gate over past Saddleback?" Pierce asked as he dismounted. His boots landed on a thin layer of day-old crunchy snow, a far cry from the three-foot drifts he'd steered clear of at higher elevations.

"The one leading to the BLM land? What were you doing all the way out there?"

"Just looking around, getting a feel for things again. It's been a while, you know."

"What about the gate?"

"The chain's cut."

Jamie's brow wrinkled. "That's odd."

"I thought so, too." Pierce tried to catch a

glimpse of who might be inside the chopper. "I wish I knew who the hell we were standing here to greet."

"Maybe I should take off and see about that gate." The old guy was happier in a saddle than on the ground.

"Stick around," Pierce said, handing Jamie the pinto's reins. "These people won't be here long, not when I explain about the storm."

"Speaking of that storm, I sent a few of the men to the higher pastures to bring the heifers closer to the ranch. Those first-time mothers need help now and again."

Pierce nodded. He understood Jamie was keeping him in the loop and he appreciated it, but except for that chain being cut, there wasn't a thing he could tell Jamie that Jamie didn't already know.

Pierce had taken a dozen steps onto the field when he heard another engine and turned to see the arrival of a ranch vehicle. The young driver looked sullen as though being asked to transport visitors was beneath him.

The sound of the helicopter door opening reclaimed Pierce's attention and he turned in time to see a man jump out of the chopper. Dressed in black from the sunglasses plastered on an expressionless face to the leather coat strained across burly shoulders, he scanned the field like a vulture, shaved bald head reflecting what little light fought its way through the gloom. Other than the old hangar, which housed the ranch helicopter, and a wind sock whipping around as the weather picked up, there wasn't a heck of a lot to see.

Which begged the question in Pierce's head: What was he doing standing out here in the frickin' cold, waiting for a bad version of Mr. T to give the place a once-over? He took a deep breath of icy air. "Welcome to—"

"Stop right there," the man growled.

Pierce felt his forehead furrow. "Excuse me?"

"I said stop. Let me see some ID."

The corners of Pierce's lips lifted. "You're kidding, right? You land on private property and then go ordering me around? Who *are* you?"

At that moment, a child appeared in the open door of the chopper. Hands from inside reached as if to detain him, but the boy slipped away easily, hitting the ground with a thud and taking off at a sprint, his face split with a big old grin.

All things considered, he was an astonishing-looking kid. About eight or so, bright red hair, decked out in a buckskin jacket, cowboy boots, spurs and two tin six-shooters that banged against his skinny legs as he ran. A blue cowboy hat flew out behind him, tethered by a cord around his neck.

The bald man tried a full body block, but the

kid was wily and darted away until he all but slammed into Pierce's legs.

"Whoa, partner," Pierce said, catching the small shoulders in his hands, ignoring the twinge in his heart. Eight. That's about how old Patrick would have been.

The child looked up at him with silver dollar eyes. "Are you a *real* cowboy?" he said.

Behind them, Jamie snickered and Pierce threw him a dirty look. To the boy, he said, "Of course I'm a real cowboy." He looked the kid over and added, "From the size of those spurs, so are you."

He glanced up from the child in time to see an older man with deep lines running down pale, gaunt cheeks standing at the chopper door. He wore a fur cap and military-looking wool coat over what appeared to be a uniform and stood like a conquering hero awaiting a ticker-tape parade. Upon making eye contact with Pierce, he nodded curtly, but when he hit the ground, he made his way toward the bald man who was in the process of slipping a very small derringer into his jacket pocket.

Pierce smiled. Not exactly the kind of weapon he would have pegged the big guy to carry. Soon the men were deep in conversation, smoke from the bodyguard's burning cigarette wreathing their heads.

"I have six-shooters, too," the boy said, looking up at Pierce.

Was it possible Cody had set him up for some elaborate joke? "What in the daylights is going on?" he grumbled.

"Beats me," Jamie murmured from behind him.

"Cody didn't tell you anything about this?"

"Like I keep telling you, he said nothing."

Movement at the chopper door signaled another newcomer. This was beginning to remind Pierce of a clown car at the circus where characters kept popping out, each more bizarre than the one before.

That comparison flew out the window as a woman wearing a white hooded jacket nipped in at the waist stepped onto the field. As she pushed back the hood, shiny ebony hair cascaded to her shoulders.

The woman paused as if to assess the situation and then immediately began walking toward Pierce and the boy.

At first he was just mesmerized by her long, slender legs and the curves the tight jacket couldn't conceal. But the closer she got the more his gaze zeroed in on her face. Damn near aqua eyes, the color of an alpine lake and just as clear. Lips full, beautifully curved, painted red. Skin that wasn't really skin; it couldn't be. It had to be satin or silk.

There was something about her that seemed familiar. Had he seen her on the cover of a magazine near a supermarket checkout lane? It had been a while since he'd been in a movie theater, but if she was an actress and these people were in the movie business, it might explain things.

"You must be Cody," she said, extending a cashmere-covered hand. Her accented voice held the tiniest trace of an edge as though she was exerting a lot of effort into sounding casual.

"No," he said, taking her hand, "my brother was called away. I'm Pierce Westin. And you are—"

"Hold it!" the older man called and immediately strode across the field toward them. The hulk stayed behind. "I thought we agreed you would wait inside the chopper until we establish security. I'm informed this man will not show his ID."

"Why the hell should I show you my ID?" Pierce said evenly. "Seems to me it ought to be the other way around."

"You don't expect trouble here, do you?" the woman asked, glancing left and right, those beautiful eyes suddenly flooded with anxiety. She withdrew her hand from Pierce's grasp and anchored it in front of her chest with the other.

"After Seattle, I expect trouble everywhere which is why I made sure you have a new bodyguard." The older man nodded at the bald guy. Then, with thin lips pressed together, he shifted his hooded gaze to Pierce.

Beautiful woman and interesting undercurrents aside, this was all just too bizarre. "Listen, folks," Pierce said calmly, "this has been…well, interesting, anyway, but there's a storm approaching. I don't know what kind of deal you made with Cody, but I don't have time to—"

"There isn't a doubt in my mind you're one of Melissa Browning's sons," the woman said. "You look just like her. Same dark hair, same gray eyes."

"You know my mother?"

"No, not exactly, but I do see you bear a striking resemblance."

She had dazzled him with her looks, aroused his curiosity with a couple of telltale signs of apprehension, but to hear her accented voice speak his mother's name—her maiden name at that—just kicked it all into overdrive. "How in the world do you know what my mother looks like?"

"I've upset you," she said softly.

"Nothing about her can upset me," he said as his gut clenched. Liar…

"I'm so relieved. Actually, I saw a photograph of her taken when she was young."

He stepped back a few inches. "Who are you? What are you and all these other people doing here?"

She rested her hands on the boy's shoulders. "This is my cousin, Toby."

"No, Analise," the child protested, looking up at her. "You promised you'd call me Tex."

She smiled down at him. "My mistake, Tex. And this gentleman—" here she nodded at the older man "—is General Kaare. I am Analise Emille." She frowned, her forehead wrinkling just a little, her luscious lips slightly puckered. "You weren't expecting us?"

"Not exactly," he admitted. "See, Cody didn't say much before he…left."

The aqua eyes widened. For a second he wondered if she and his brother were fooling around, then he remembered she hadn't known Pierce wasn't Cody until he'd announced it. Besides, Cody was still married and he wasn't the kind of man to get involved with another woman even if he and his wife were estranged.

"Princess Analise," the general said smoothly. "Let's at least get you out of the open."

"Princess?" Pierce said softly as the woman reacted to the general's warning by flinching.

When she met Pierce's gaze again, she tried a smile but it looked forced. "You didn't know that, either, did you?"

Chapter Two

"Princess of what exactly?" For the moment, Pierce let the "out of the open" comment slide.

"Of Chatioux, of course," the general growled. "Surely you recognize King Thomas's youngest child, Analise Elsbeth Emille."

So that explained the accent. He'd heard of Chatioux—it was one of those little countries tucked somewhere in Northern Europe. As he tried to make sense of a genuine princess visiting the Open Sky Ranch, another man and a middle-aged woman stepped out of the helicopter. They both threw curious glances toward the princess but scurried to the waiting truck, hunkered inside their coats as if freezing. The ranch hand opened doors for them and they climbed inside. Meanwhile, the helicopter pilot began emptying the external luggage bins, piling trunks and cases on the field.

Pierce turned around and caught Jamie's eyes.

Jamie shrugged and shook his head. Even the horses looked confused.

"Your brother requested we keep our group small," the general announced. "The princess and her cousin, one bodyguard, the princess's attendant, Mr. Vaughn and myself. Six, that is all. We left double that number behind at the hotel in Jackson Hole."

Pierce ran a gloved hand over his jaw. What the hell was he supposed to do with royalty in March on a cattle ranch? This was insane and he found himself itching to ask his usually predictable brother what in the world he'd been thinking.

Maybe the ranch was losing money and had started taking paying guests... Maybe Adam's push into organic beef wasn't panning out the way everyone hoped it would...

Man, if that was true, did his dad know? Impossible to wrap his brain around the old man agreeing to turn the Open Sky into a damn dude ranch.

"Let me explain something," Pierce began. "If you get caught in the weather system that's coming, you might end up in Wyoming for days. Considering the fact Cody isn't here as planned and I wasn't expecting people of your stature, it would be best to reschedule your visit. I'll see about a refund—"

"I don't understand," the princess said. "Refund of what?"

"If you paid something up front—"

"Paid!" the general barked. "We do not pay!"

Okay, so there was no money involved. That wasn't it. "Sorry," Pierce said. "I just assumed—"

"It seems your brother kept his word to say nothing of our identity," the general added. "That kind of honor is admirable. I should liked to have met him."

"Exactly," Pierce said. "And that's why it would be best all around if you people leave now and reschedule a visit for after Cody gets home. We'll just get your stuff back in the chopper and—"

"But I want to stay," the boy cried in panic. He looked longingly toward Jamie who with his bowed legs and ancient chaps did look the part of a real cowboy. "Look how big the brown horse is and it has a white star on its forehead just like the one in my book. Can we have a campfire with real grub?"

"It's twenty-three degrees out here," Pierce said.

The princess touched his arm and turned her back to the others. He turned with her. She took a few steps and he followed. "I understand your reservations about hosting us, Mr. Westin, I really do," she said in a voice barely above a whisper but it sure traveled through his body like a hot tornado. "I can't explain right now why it's so important for us to stay for just a day, but will you trust me that it is? Please? And, well, it means so much to my cousin."

Pierce took a deep breath as he gazed into her eyes. Not a movie star, not a paying guest, just a beautiful princess with a quiver in her voice as if denying her would crush her. He glanced back at the little boy who appeared damn close to crying.

Cripes.

"If it's money—" she began.

"No, no," he said. "It's not money." It was on the tip of his tongue to ask her what she was afraid of and if that's why she needed to stay on the ranch but he didn't. For now it would suffice that it was important to her—hell, be honest, what else did he have to do for the next twenty-four hours that was any more important than giving aid and, dare he hope, comfort to a gorgeous woman? "We have an indoor arena," he said at last. "I guess we could build a campfire in there."

"Oh, thank you," Princess Analise said with an exhaled breath.

"Could we bring a cow inside?" the child asked hopefully. He'd obviously been eavesdropping.

"Why not?" Pierce said, lips twitching.

"Can we also visit the very small house we flew over?"

"The very small house?"

"Over there," he said, pointing east.

"The ice-fishing shanty," Jamie volunteered. He'd apparently moved closer when the child had the good sense to compliment Jamie's favorite mare. "Adam painted it yellow last fall. You folks must have seen that."

"Adam?"

"My other brother."

"That's right, I forgot. There are three of you, right?"

And how did she know that? "Yeah. Three."

"The fishing shanty did look interesting from the air," she said, adding, "though it's very remote. I would love to see what it's like inside. At home, ours are sometimes quite charming."

"I doubt this one would qualify as charming," Pierce said.

"I'll show it to you, ma'am," Jamie offered, a slight blush creeping up his wrinkled neck. "And as far as a campfire, we built a big old covered pavilion a couple of years ago for Cody's wedding. It's got gas heaters and everything."

"That sounds perfect," Princess Analise said.

Seeing the ranch hand had started piling their luggage in the back of the truck, Pierce strode over and hefted a couple of suitcases. The sooner they got going, the sooner he'd find out what was really going on. Being back in Wyoming was not his idea of a great time. Being with a very attractive woman who just happened to be a little scared and a little nervous and needed his shoulder to cry on—well, that was right up his alley.

"I am going to have an adventure!" the boy cried. "You, too, Cousin Analise."

"The kid is just like you were, Pierce," Jamie called. "Always ready for action. Hell's bells, I'd wager you're still like that."

Pierce shook his head as he dumped the last of the luggage in the truck. By now the helicopter engines had once again engaged. The general tried herding the princess and the boy to the idling vehicle but they both hung back near Jamie as the chopper rose into the air and the horses danced around a little but not much. They were used to the ranch aircraft.

How had a princess from a small country half a world away become familiar with a photograph of Pierce's long missing mother? Was it possible Princess Analise knew where Melissa Browning Westin was now? Is that why Cody had agreed to this visit?

If so, why had his older brother left almost on the eve of her arrival and without so much as a word hinting at who was coming and why?

Pierce pushed his hat back on his head. "The truck only seats six, and what with the driver, I guess someone will have to ride back with Jamie or me." Looking over at the bald man dressed in black, he raised his voice and added, "I guess you're it, buddy."

But Toby had already run over to Jamie and put a hand on the mare's glistening brown neck. "I want to ride this one. Is her name Star? May I, please?"

Jamie chuckled. "I can take the little fella," he said. "Come on, son, up you go."

"And I will ride with you," Princess Analise announced, looking Pierce straight in the eye. He smiled at her. Fine by him but her announcement seemed to have galvanized the bodyguard who approached like a belligerent bull.

The general sputtered. "But, Princess. It is hardly necessary or appropriate for you to ride with this man. Nor is it safe—"

"Nevertheless, I will ride with him," she said, and there was a change in the timbre of her voice that stopped the bodyguard dead in his tracks and shut down the general.

The corner of Pierce's upper lip lifted. Nice to see the princess square her shoulders and jut her chin. He climbed back in the saddle and, freeing a stirrup for her use, extended a hand and pulled her up behind him, smiling to himself as her hands landed on his waist.

"You will be cautious," the general said, gaze darting between Pierce and the princess.

"Sure," Pierce said.

Before he could turn the horse, the general caught the bridle. "Once we have suitable accommodations, you will explain what precautions you've taken to protect the princess."

There it was—the dead fish in the punch bowl, the issue everyone had been skirting around since they landed. The pushy bodyguard, the flustered general, a princess looking over her shoulder...

"You know, maybe it's about time someone tells me exactly what she needs protection from," Pierce said.

The general raised gray eyebrows. "From whoever is intent on killing her, of course."

Chapter Three

Analise tightened her grip on Pierce as he turned his head slightly and said, "Someone is trying to kill you?"

She cringed at the theatrics of the general's statement though there was more than a grain of truth behind it. "Yes," she said.

"No wonder the general looked jumpy when you announced you were leaving him and the bodyguard behind."

"The general is a very old and trusted friend of my father's, but I'm a twenty-six-year-old adult and his hovering gets on my nerves." She instantly regretted speaking out. The general was the general. He was not the reason she was nervous and not the reason she'd insisted on riding with Pierce.

The past week had passed in a blur as she did her best to pretend she wasn't worried about death threats or arriving at this ranch. Twenty-four hours from now, this would be over. Well, at least part of it would.

She took a few deep breaths of blessedly un-recirculated air and concentrated on the moment. The sway of the horse, the faint smell of the pines. The low growl of the truck rumbling behind them. The solid feel of the man whose back she hugged.

He did resemble the photo she'd seen of his mother, but in a masculine way. At least six feet tall, broad shoulders, gorgeous slate eyes and strong features, a sensuous mouth. Even through the padding of a winter coat, she could tell he was fit and muscular.

As for the glint in his eyes and the deep voice? Those were masculine, too. Intimidating, per-haps, but in a way that made her feel protected. He looked competent, more than able to take care of himself and anyone else for that matter.

These thoughts brought up images of the man she was expected to marry next year, a Chatioux nobleman of some distinction. He and Pierce Westin were both in their mid-thirties, but there all similarities ended.

She wouldn't think about Ricard right now. She had the rest of her life to do that.

"Let's talk about who's trying to kill you," Pierce said, glancing over his shoulder again, the flash of his eyes surprisingly warm. "Is this person the reason you came to the ranch? Are you here for refuge?"

"No, I made arrangements to come here months ago and this situation is relatively new."

"Months ago and Cody never told anyone? That's pretty amazing."

A little flutter in her throat kept her from responding immediately. She'd insisted on riding with him to have the privacy in which to reveal the true nature of her visit. Allowing herself to get sidetracked would squander the opportunity.

"Princess? You still back there?"

"I want to explain why I begged you to let us stay—"

"And I'd like to hear it," he interrupted. "But first tell me about the would-be assassins just in case your general is right and one is hiding behind those rocks over there with a howitzer. Start with what you were doing in Seattle."

She glanced at the rocks, then shook her head. "We were attending an environmental symposium."

"And someone tried to do what? Shoot you, shove you in front of a bus?"

"Nothing so direct. Two days ago I received an anonymous note. It warned that if I valued my life, I would convince my father to vote against the natural-gas pipeline proposed for Chatioux. There was no way to respond, but I could have told the writer that while my father will weigh my opinion, in the end will do what is best for our country. He would never put family over duty."

"He sounds like my father," Pierce said.

"Are you close to your father?"

"Not exactly," Pierce said. "I've been back here three days and I think we've spent all of ten minutes in each other's company."

"Why? What happened between you?"

He laughed but the sound held little humor. "Don't try wiggling out of your story by trying to uncover mine. When does the king vote?"

"In five days. The parliament is divided so my father's vote will be the deciding factor."

"And how is he leaning?"

"Construction of the pipeline would bring in much-needed revenue. Our country is in the middle of great flux. There aren't enough jobs to keep our young people employed and they immigrate elsewhere in alarming numbers. We import too many things and export too few. This weakens us socially as well as economically and that puts our national security at risk. It's all interconnected and Russia would love to see us crumble."

She sighed again. "The bottom line is this pipeline would make the difference between a brighter, safer future and a continuing spiral downward resulting in citizen unrest if not out-and-out war on our borders. If environmental concerns can be met, my father has no choice but to embrace it."

"Can these concerns be met?"

"Yes."

"And that's what you'll tell him?"

"Of course. But Mr. Vaughn doesn't agree with me."

"Mr. Vaughn. He's the diplomat who scurried to the car with the skulking woman?"

"The woman is Bierta, my personal maid. Mr. Vaughn was Chatioux's official delegate to the symposium. I was unofficial. He wants everything to stay as it has always been. He claims it's because of the environment, but I don't know, he's kind of odd. And since these threats started, he's worried he'll be standing too close if someone tries to kill me."

Pierce muttered, "It doesn't sound like your father trusts this Vaughn fellow's opinion or he wouldn't have asked you to go and act as his ears."

"My father is a thorough man, a good king. I have ordered everyone to keep this threat a secret from him until after the vote. I do not want him put in the position of having to choose."

She didn't add why. Her father's declining health was not known outside the family.

"The general alluded to something that happened in Seattle. Was this separate from the threatening note?"

"Yes," she said, the memory of the attack once again vibrant and chilling.

The horse started down a dip in the road and Analise slid forward against Pierce's back. It was impossible not to have some body contact, but she did her best to keep it minimal. Forced closer than before, she suddenly noticed the way his hair waved against the back of his neck, right above his collar, dark against his skin, fine and tender-looking. He appeared to have a tan.

"Princess?"

She blinked a couple of times as the horse began the climb to the other side of the gully. Her grip tightened around his waist. "On the last day of the symposium, my driver didn't show up to transport us between hotel and convention center. Mr. Vaughn had rented a car, so he offered to drive but he got terribly lost. We ended up in a bad area of town in a narrow alley where people seemed to be living. Claude, my bodyguard from home, got out of the car when a group of men started **pushing** at it." Analise paused. Her pitch had risen as she spoke, the words tumbling one after the other.

"There was a terrible fight. They broke poor Claude's arm in two places. He had to stay in the hospital so the general hired a new man from an American agency to fill in."

"The charmer I met at the airstrip?"

"Not so charming."

"Are you saying that because he's actually said or done something suspicious or because he glowers all the time?"

"I think it's the glowering. Plus, I had to ask him twice not to smoke in front of my cousin. Toby is allergic."

"Anything else happen in Seattle?"

"That's all, I guess. Claude was hurt but I was never even threatened. I don't see how any of it could have been planned. We were simply lost. Mr. Vaughn was as terrified by the events as I was."

"I'm kind of surprised he joined you for this leg of your trip," Pierce said. "He sounds like the kind of guy who would have preferred staying in a plush room back in the city."

"I was surprised, too. But he insisted he wanted to see something besides hotel rooms and on behalf of goodwill, I relented."

"And what about your cousin? Did you really take a little kid to a symposium on the environment?"

"Of course not. He was visiting his Canadian grandparents during spring break. It was prearranged that he would join my entourage for the journey back to Chatioux and the visit to the ranch."

Pierce was silent for a few moments before he mumbled to himself.

"Did you say something?" she asked, unconsciously pressing against his broad back. She lowered her voice, looked ahead of him down the road where she could barely see the dark shape of the brown horse carrying Toby. "Is something wrong? Did you see something?"

"Just a second," he said, and yanked the reins to the right. The pinto climbed the rocky bank, cresting a ridge pocketed with drifts of snow left over from the last storm. Below them, the truck slowed and its windows rolled down.

Analise held on tight to Pierce's coat, unsure what was going on. It crossed her mind that perhaps she'd been wrong, that perhaps this wasn't Cody Westin's brother, that he was an imposter, working for whomever had written that disturbing note.

"Go on ahead of us," Pierce yelled as the truck on the road below rolled to a stop.

"Absolutely not," the general cried from the front passenger window. The bodyguard glared through the back window.

"The engine noise is bothering the horse," Pierce said.

"We will not leave," the general announced.

"Tell them to go ahead," Pierce said softly over his shoulder. Analise, on the verge of slipping off the horse and running for the truck, raised a hand instead and called, "It's okay."

General Kaare looked furious but the driver sped up and the truck soon pulled ahead.

After a few moments, they traveled back down the rise to the road. The vehicle was a good hundred yards away by then, disappearing around a curve. By now the attack of nerves that had gripped her a few moments before was gone and Analise sagged.

"You okay back there?" Pierce asked.

"Yes. Of course. The horse wasn't really bothered, was he?"

"No. I was."

"Me, too."

This time his profile came with a furrowed brow under the brim of his hat. "How do you live like this, Princess?"

"Like what?"

"Like a beautiful fish in a crystal bowl."

Had he just called her beautiful? She smiled against his back, unexplainably pleased. She was used to having people fawn over her, accustomed to reading flattering things about her appearance in magazines and newspapers, but it was different coming from him. "I guess a person gets used to whatever it is they've known," she finally said.

"Anyway, I went to school in England for several years, so I'm not always guarded so closely."

He put a hand over hers as it rested against his flat stomach. "I don't mean to alarm you, but I have to admit your story about what happened in Seattle worries me."

"It worried the general, too, but he wouldn't discuss it. Will you?"

"It sounds like a setup."

"Excuse me?" she said, and this time her gaze darted behind them. She hadn't realized until that moment how the car had provided a safety net at her back and now that it was gone, she felt naked.

"The missing driver, the sudden offer of a ride, the knot of threatening men, the attack on your bodyguard, a new man hired—it sounds like a setup with one express goal—get rid of Claude. How well do you know this man, Vaughn?"

"Not very well."

He squeezed her hand with his. She'd felt his strength when he helped her mount the horse; she felt it in his body now when he shifted his weight with the ride. Power. But not the overbearing affectations of the general. No, something more subtle and quiet and substantial.

"I'll keep an eye on him," he added. "And on you."

"Oh, please, not another eye. There are already so many!"

"It's not just you," he said.

"What do you mean?"

"I mean for the time being I'm responsible for everything that happens on this ranch. I want to hand it back to Cody and Adam and my dad in one piece and that means no trouble."

"Then you don't normally live here?"

"No."

"Do you have a ranch somewhere else? Is someone taking care of that while you are here? A wife, perhaps?" The pinto picked up his pace as the road ascended and the distant roof of a building came into sight. Just like the horses at home in Chatioux, this one apparently knew when the stable was close by.

"Why, Princess," Pierce said, flashing a grin over his shoulder, "is that your way of finding out if I'm single?"

She'd been thinking more along the lines of establishing his identity. For some reason, it seemed unlikely an assassin would claim a family.

Wait. Did she really think this was some kind of setup? If she had, wouldn't she have insisted the car stay behind them? *Trust your instincts, Analise,* her father had said on more than one occasion. *Sometimes that's all the armor you'll have...*

"You're wearing gloves," she said evenly. "A woman likes to know these things."

"So does a man," he said without turning.

"I'm about to become engaged."

"That's too bad."

"And you?"

"I'm not engaged or married or involved with anyone at the moment."

"But you have been?"

"All those things at one time or another," he said and there was a tone to his voice that added, *Once was enough.*

"So if you aren't a rancher, what are you?"

"I'm part owner of a sort of security outfit," he said, but there'd been a brief pause before his answer.

"Are you like a policeman?"

"Not really. We help businesses track down inner-corporate ne'er-do-wells."

"I see."

"You do?"

"Like industrial espionage," she said.

"Yes. My partner tends to take the computer angle. I get more hands-on."

Analise looked ahead and caught sight of a huge log house. Shaped like an inverted V with wings, it appeared to rise to three stories in the middle with tall glass windows. Slender, graceful white-barked trees, their branches currently bare, cradled the upper stories. The long walkway leading to the front was built of rock. A partial roof supported by huge peeled logs covered the end closest to the house. Additional structures could be glimpsed fanning out at the back and there appeared to be a small pond, frozen over, that surrounded the patio on the north end.

When they'd flown overhead, she'd seen long barns with red roofs she supposed held feed and others that must house large equipment. The fields had been dotted with hundreds of black cows, so stark against the winter ground. Add rolling hillsides, millions of evergreen trees and miles of fences and the overall impression was of prosperity.

"You must have enjoyed growing up here," she said, leaning forward to peer over his shoulder and unconsciously inhaling the clean male scent of his skin. Coming from the privileged life she'd led, admiring a lifestyle wasn't something she had occasion to do often. But there was a sense of freedom and openness about the place that was foreign to her—and appealing.

For a second she wished she was here alone with Pierce. Just the two of them riding this horse. He was a stranger—he'd never even heard of her before today, he had no expectations, no preconceived ideas of what she was supposed to be.

In fact, if she was honest, she would admit the thought of being alone with a strong, attractive man whose only interest in her was fleeting and trivial was a real turn-on. He wasn't the kind of man she could ever be with and that was exciting, too.

"The house is bigger now than it used to be. Cody did some serious remodeling before he married Cassie."

"Is she here now or is she away with him?"

"Neither. The marriage didn't last, she ran off, á la my mother."

Analise was willing to bet his casual tone covered some pretty intense undercurrents. "And your other brother, Adam?"

"Off hiking. If you mean is he married, the answer is no. He's waiting for some nice, shy farm girl to wander into his life." He turned in the saddle as he reined the horse to a halt and added, "I'd like to talk to you about that photo you mentioned."

"I'd like to talk to you, too," she said, nerves flaring again. How much should she tell him? She'd been directed to divulge as little as possible. That had seemed doable when she spoke with Pierce's brother on the phone months before. With this man?

The key would be saying enough to garner his help without giving anything away....

Chapter Four

Pierce looked over his shoulder again. "I'm assuming the photo ties into that 'important' reason for your visit," he added.

"Yes," she said. "I tried to tell you earlier—"

"As we rode, I know. But I want to look you in the eyes when you talk."

"Why? Do you think I would lie?"

"I didn't say that."

"Then what—"

"Words aren't the only way a person speaks," he said, "and sometimes the way something isn't said is pretty informative."

She blinked a few times as she thought about that statement. "It may be hard to get time alone again," she warned as he stopped the horse next to the walkway.

"I'll figure it out." He got off the horse, stepped onto the walkway and reached up to help her dismount. The next thing she knew, she was sliding down his firm body, his strong hands gripping her waist, his breath warm where it touched her bare skin. Her feet hit the rocks a second later and she looked up at him, peered into the depths of his eyes, and felt a shock as something almost tangible passed between them.

And in that moment she knew she could trust him with her concerns. Not everything, of course, and certainly not with her heart.

What an odd thing to think.

"Princess? You are all right?" the general called, and she and Pierce both turned to find the older man marching toward them, moving faster than normal.

General Kaare was old-school. Royals should be admired but never touched by a mere mortal like Pierce Westin.

Ignoring his question, she looked around the open meadow. "Where's Toby?"

"I am told he is out in the barn with the cowboys. Your maid is inside getting your rooms ready for occupancy. Mr. Vaughn was cold—I believe he's inside by the fireplace being attended by the staff. Come now, come inside." The general's eyes lingered on Pierce's hands which still encircled her waist.

"What about her bodyguard?" Pierce asked as he kept his hands right where they were. "Where is he?"

"Patrolling the immediate vicinity, getting the

lay of the land, or so he called it. Come, Princess."

Something cold touched Analise's cheek and she looked up as another flake landed on her forehead.

Holding her hands palms up, she watched the flakes swirling overhead before landing on the blue cashmere. "Is this your storm?"

"No, this isn't the storm," Pierce said, his eyes delving into hers. At last he moved his hands—on his terms, she noticed with a touch of amusement. "These are just stray flakes. I'll be inside after I get Sam to the stable."

"Let your staff take care of that," the general demanded as he straightened the lapels on his coat. "We must discuss—"

"My staff?" Pierce repeated with a sudden glint in his eyes. "This isn't a castle with servants, General. Around here, a man takes care of his own horse. I'll be with you in a few minutes." With that, he swung himself back into the saddle and trotted off toward a large structure to the south.

Analise smiled into her jacket collar.

"The man is impudent," the Colonel snapped. "He is much too familiar with you. Furthermore…"

"General? We are guests in his home."

"And why exactly is that?" the general asked,

leveling hooded eyes at her. "Why are we here, Princess Analise? After the situation in Seattle, why didn't we skip this frivolous side trip and return to Chatioux as I suggested? I know your father—"

"We are here because *I* want to be here," she interrupted, affecting the aristocratic manner she knew would remind him not to push too hard or too far.

He studied her intently for a moment. "Then, Princess, let me say this. Without information and in such a remote spot, I am powerless to protect you." He held up a hand to still her as she started to comment. "Furthermore, it is clear you've placed your trust in this cowboy, this stranger. So be it." He bowed his head slightly and gestured toward the house with one large hand. Analise preceded him down the walkway.

PIERCE SPENT THE next hour getting Sam settled and delegating work. He put men on duty creating something approaching a campout in the pavilion Jamie mentioned. He sent another up to replace the lock on the violated gate in Shadow Canyon, and turned over babysitting chores to Jamie to whom Toby had taken an instant liking. Even now the child was perched atop the mare as Jamie led her around the indoor arena, Cody's yellow Lab trotting along while expertly avoiding hooves.

The dog was kind of an odd choice of breed for a ranch. For the first time, Pierce wondered where she'd come from.

The kid spied Pierce and waved vigorously, slipping in the big saddle when he took one of his hands off the horn. Pierce waved back before the boy fell, and turned away, a bitter taste in the back of his mouth as Patrick once again flitted across his mind.

The next thirty minutes were spent in a frustrating string of dropped calls to his partner at Westin-Turner. Bob Turner was an old army buddy and a good friend, but lately he'd been discontent. Pierce thought he knew why—it was Sue, Bob's girlfriend, and she was exerting pressure on him to settle down.

The ranch hand who had driven the truck to the airstrip and back showed up as Pierce was leaving the barn, the Lab close on his heels. The man had a familiar look to him but he was far too young to have worked here in the days Pierce was around all the time. "You one of Tom Garvey's boys?" Pierce asked.

"Yeah. I'm Lucas."

Pierce offered his hand and they shook. Lucas was in his early twenties, sandy-colored hair, blue-eyed and wiry like all the Garvey men, no doubt strong as an ox despite it. He had a pointed chin and nose and about three days' growth of beard which didn't really amount to much. "I went to school with your older brother, Doyle."

"Yeah, I know," Lucas said. He shoved both hands in his pockets.

"How is Doyle?"

"He's okay," Lucas said, but his eyes shut down. Too late Pierce remembered Cody saying something in one of their phone calls about Adam firing Doyle last winter. Something about temper issues, a fight that broke another man's nose. Though no formal charges were ever filed, Doyle had left and everyone knew why.

Pierce and Doyle had been adversaries in high school. Both of them had been screw-ups, but while Pierce's antics had been confined to victimless rowdiness, Doyle's had landed him in juvie. The boy was as mean and sneaky as his father, the elder Garvey.

Well, that was in the past. Pierce quickly changed the subject.

"For the next twenty-four hours, I want you to be a kind of unofficial bodyguard for our guests, especially Princess Analise," he said. "Just keep an eye on things around the ranch. Report anything unusual to me. And later on, when we have the cookout, stick close by. I'll find someone else to help you."

"How about Darrell Cox?"

"The big guy with all the freckles? Sure, he'd be fine."

"I'll tell him."

"Thanks," Pierce said and took off for the house, the dog running ahead. After he called his assistant back on the land line, his plan was to get some answers from Princess Analise.

And that brought her fully back to mind. He rebuilt her face, then the feel of her seated behind him on the horse, especially when she'd bumped up against his back. That led to reviewing the second she'd spent sliding down his body when she dismounted and the rush of heat that had passed through him, the frisson like a nuclear reactor that had zapped him when their gazes met and held.

He tried to remember the details of the last woman he'd been serious about. Okay, maybe *serious about* wasn't the right criteria. Maybe he needed to de-escalate to *hot for*.

A noise stopped him midway across the pasture that passed for a yard and he looked up in time to see Pauline, the Open Sky housekeeper, entering the house through the kitchen door, a yellow dish towel draped over her arm, the Lab underfoot.

In the next instant, a long forgotten memory hit Pierce with such force it stopped him midstep.

His mother on that porch. Back before the fancy rockwork, back before the big A-frame addition. Standing there with a black fry pan and a metal spoon, banging them together, wearing a yellow checked shirt so vibrant it was like a flag on a drag strip.

And just like that, another memory. His father, walking beside him, looking up at the noise and grinning, laughing at the clatter, slapping Pierce on the back in the process.

The memory was so real that for a moment the house before him seemed to shrink and so did he, flying back through the years into the body of his five-year-old self, the feel of his father's good-natured thump thundering across his shoulders.

Pierce's foot hitting the ground jarred the images clear out of his head. They'd been so real it took him a second to figure out what had happened.

And then he plucked the hat off his head and threw it to the ground. What was he doing here? He was supposed to be in Italy, not riding around on horses and babysitting royalty. And now he was having memories of his mother who had abandoned the whole damn family?

Who said, "You can't go home again"? Thomas Wolfe? Well, the man was a genius, it was true.

He snagged his hat off the ground. The black

felt was covered with snowflakes and that startled him; he hadn't even noticed it coming down
that hard. Glancing at the small one-story cabin
where his father had exiled himself while his leg
healed from a busted kneecap, he shoved the hat
back on, grimacing as the cold brim settled on
his forehead. If his old man got whiff there was
a woman here with possible news of his long lost
wife, he'd blow a gasket.

Crap.

Pierce put his head down and continued walking. Time to reassure General Kaare security
was under control. Then he'd find out what the
princess knew about his mother so he could take
the past and put it where it belonged—behind
him.

Way behind him.

ANALISE LIKED THE room she'd been given. The
green-and-yellow color scheme complemented
the honey-gold of the log walls, evoking spring
even in the midst of foul weather. It was big, too.
Maybe too big. In her present state of mind she
would have preferred a windowless, one-door
closet, but at least there wasn't a balcony.

There was only one photo displayed and it
was a wedding picture of a man and a woman
on horseback, her in a billowing white gown,
him sitting tall in the saddle. It was hard to see

the particulars of their faces. All Analise could really tell was that the man looked a lot like Pierce, only darker, and the woman had very long blond hair. Oh, and that they were smiling.

Was this Pierce's sister-in-law's room? Was this his brother? It had to be. They looked so happy! What could have happened to ruin it for them?

The concept of leaving someone to whom you were obligated and with whom you had exchanged vows was so foreign to Analise that she couldn't puzzle it out even though she knew half the world did it all the time.

While Bierta, her maid, opened suitcases and shook out clothes—way too many of them in Analise's opinion; honestly, a ball gown? Two tiaras? Here?—Analise leaned against the log walls and peered through the large window. Though she stood at a distance from the glass she could see the snow had picked up and as she watched, a man walked out of a distant building, a pale dog rushing ahead toward the house.

Even from this distance she could tell it was Pierce and her lips curved. He stopped midway across the yard and stood there a long second, then threw his hat on the ground, swept it from the snow and pulled it back on his head.

She turned away.

"Tea, ma'am?" Bierta asked, standing close by

and holding a tray on which sat a steaming cup of herb tea she'd brewed from the hot water she brought along in a thermos.

"Thank you," Analise said as she perched on the edge of an upholstered chair.

Bierta, who couldn't have been a day over forty, was a dowdy woman with brown hair and small, dark eyes that swam behind thick lenses. Her uniform was dark blue, her sensible shoes brown, and she moved with deliberate steps.

"Wouldn't you like some tea, as well?"

"Oh, no, Princess," Bierta said, looking downright scandalized by the suggestion she join the princess for a beverage. "I'm not the one who requires relaxation, ma'am. You're the one whose very life is in danger. When I think of what could have happened to you in that alley if poor Claude hadn't sacrificed himself for you, it makes me—" She stopped herself short and shuddered.

Analise put the cup down on the neighboring table so abruptly tea spilled over the lip onto the saucer.

"I heard the general talking to Mr. Vaughn," Bierta continued, lowering her voice. "He said *you* were the target, that someone was trying to steal you away, that if they'd succeeded they would have had to kill you to remain safe themselves because your father wouldn't rest until—"

"Please, Bierta," Analise said firmly. "I don't

want to hear any more of this. We're all a little unnerved after, well, everything. I'd like to be alone for a while."

"Are you sure that's wise?" Bierta said, managing to give the impression that murderers were lurking behind the cheery curtains. "We're in the middle of nowhere here, if you'll pardon me saying, Princess. The wilds. There could be a gunman on the prowl—"

"You're going to have to fill in as Toby's nanny," Analise interrupted. "His things undoubtedly need unpacking."

It took a few minutes, but Bierta finally closed the door behind her. Sighing, Analise got up from the chair and moved to the mirror. She picked up her hairbrush and ran it through the gentle waves, gathering it back in a silver clip. As she replaced the brush on the vanity, she heard a door close in the hall, and then another open in the other direction. Her attention caught, she stood very still and listened as footsteps approached her door. She took a step forward, waiting for whomever was out there to knock, but the footsteps stopped.

For well over a minute, she watched the knob, her heart in her throat, but it didn't turn. Was someone still out there? If so, why didn't they knock?

Swallowing hard, Analise grabbed the doorknob and pulled.

The hall was empty. A sound from the stairs had her spinning that direction in time to find Pierce stepping onto the landing.

"There you are," he said.

"Did you pass anyone on the stairs?" she asked anxiously.

"No." He narrowed his eyes. "Where's your bodyguard, Princess? Shouldn't he be standing out here, protecting you?"

Where was her bodyguard?

Pierce grabbed her arms suddenly and she blinked up at him.

"It looked like you were about to keel over," he said, his grip pressing into her sleeves and the tender flesh beneath.

She stared into his eyes for a few seconds, then shook her head. "I don't know where Harley is. Outside, I guess."

"When did you have something to eat?"

"Breakfast."

"Come on," he said, his right hand sliding down her arm to grip her hand. The motion made her quiver as she allowed herself to be pulled from the room.

Chapter Five

Pierce led Analise into the dining room where he expected to find the rest of her party eating a late lunch. The room was empty. He pushed on a swinging door and they entered the warm kitchen.

Pauline, standing at the counter, was in the process of hanging a ceramic cup on the wrought-iron mug tree Adam had made back in high school. Each big cup was bright red. Some were chipped, all were stained by coffee brewed strong enough to usher a man into the frozen predawn morning, and yet they'd been hanging in the same places for twenty years. Amazing.

The retriever sat by Pauline's legs, begging. Both Pauline and Bonnie turned at their entrance.

"Oh my, you must be the princess," Pauline gushed. "I've seen your photograph in the magazines, but you're twice as pretty in person." She managed a little self-conscious curtsey, her graying hair swinging around her face as she dipped her head. She was a good-looking sixty-something-year-old woman who had been at the ranch for at least twenty years.

The dog trotted over and sniffed Analise's hands. The princess knelt and ran her slender fingers over the animal's smooth head.

"She's a lovely dog," she said, looking up at Pauline. "Is she yours?"

"Oh, no, she's Cody's dog. Well, actually, she belonged to his wife, Cassie, but Cassie left without taking her—" Pauline put two fingers against her lips and cast Pierce a glance. "Sorry, I got to rambling…"

"It's okay," he told her. He looked at the princess and added, "Marriages have a way of turning out bad in this family." He introduced the housekeeper as the heart and soul of the Open Sky Ranch.

"I'm so pleased to have you here, Your Highness," Pauline said as Analise stood. "Your maid said you weren't to be disturbed so I didn't bring you lunch and Pierce, I was coming to see what you wanted."

"I'll take care of both of us, Pauline," Pierce said.

Pauline shook her head as she turned to the stove and took the lid off a huge pot. A wave of fragrant steam brought the heady aroma of meat and vegetables. "I can't get over how different you are," she said over her shoulder as she replaced the lid. "I mean from the boy who stormed away fifteen years ago. That boy didn't spend any time in the kitchen unless it was to eat."

"*That* boy didn't need to. He had you spoiling him rotten," Pierce said with a fond smile.

"Well, your brothers still can't cook. Might have done them both good to get out on their own for a while."

"They'll both die here with their boots on, you know that. Meanwhile, have you seen a big guy dressed in black? Sunglasses, bald, intimidating?"

"I caught a glimpse of him outside when I took your father his lunch but I haven't seen him since. I'm sure he's around somewhere. I could use some of his muscle to tote things outside for the cookout."

"I imagine much of the work for the cookout will go to you, Pauline," Princess Analise said. "I want to thank you in advance and apologize for any trouble."

"Mercy me," Pauline said, waving away the princess's concern. "We're used to coming up with meals in a hurry." She nodded at the pot on the stove. "I've already started a stew. The boys will take it out later and grill steaks and maybe hot dogs for your little cousin. We've got a big pot of beans going out there already and I'll whip up some slaw, heat loaves of bread and fry potatoes. Berry cobbler fresh from the freezer for dessert. The boys are all looking forward to it."

She took her coat off a hook by the door and shrugged it on. Looking at Pierce, she added, "If I can't help you, I'm going to go get your father's dirty dishes. Come on, Bonnie, let's go see Birch."

As soon as they'd left, Pierce put both hands on Analise's shoulders and gently pushed her down atop a stool pulled up to a huge cutting block island.

Without the distraction of a padded coat, the full force of her body kept hitting him like a two-by-four. Round breasts filled the oyster-white silk blouse styled like a Western shirt but tailored perfectly. Her jeans looked as though they'd been made just for her, maybe even sewn onto her slender hips by a half dozen hand maidens wielding needles and thread. A simple diamond flower twinkled in the sensuous hollow of her throat.

And she smelled good. Not exactly perfume, not flowery but not heavily musky, either. He had the overwhelming urge to bury his nose against her skin and inhale deeply, filling his lungs with her essence. To be truthful—he had urges that went a lot deeper than those. Good thing there was a no-trespassing sign hanging around her pretty neck or he'd have a hard time concentrating.

He turned away and opened the refrigerator. "I'm making you lunch," he announced as he gathered supplies. Unwrapping the bread Pauline had baked earlier in the day, he added, "I'd sure like to hear about that photo you mentioned."

Analise fidgeted on the stool for a minute as he sliced leftover roast beef, grown on the ranch, the product of his brother Adam's ranching techniques. Stemming his own impatience as Analise obviously sought a way to broach whatever it was she had to say, he kept quiet. She finally murmured, "Did you know your mother went to college with mine?"

"No," he said, glancing up at her as he sliced cheese. "I didn't know that."

"They were roommates as required by the school for all entering freshmen. I think because my mother was a prime minister's daughter and yours was a governor's daughter, school officials thought they would get along well."

Pierce cut the huge sandwich and placed half on his plate and half on hers. He poured two glasses of milk and handed her share over, then sat down on a stool across from her. "I know my mother went to a private university in New York, but that's about all. My grandfather died before I was born, and Mom, well, she left when I was a little kid. I haven't seen or heard from her since then."

The princes ignored the food as she leaned across the bar, hands clasped. "Our mothers became great friends," she began. "Confidantes, actually. They roomed together for several years until my mother left to go back to Chatioux to marry my father and your mother left to marry your father and come live in Wyoming."

Pierce swallowed a bite and nodded. "Okay."

"The photo I've seen many times over the years is a framed one sitting on my mother's bureau of her and your mother at school. They are both nineteen years old and look so happy and excited."

Pierce nodded again. What memories he had of his mother suggested this was an accurate description of her. He could vaguely recall lively eyes and a ready laugh. Yet as he drank the milk, he asked himself if this tenuous connection was a disappointment. Had he somewhere in the back of his head expected Analise to say she'd seen his mother relatively recently? Had he hoped for an explanation of some kind?

Of course he had.

He put the glass down and watched Analise

try to take a dainty bite of a man-size hunk of beef. "So how does this tie into you being here?"

She met his gaze. "Our mothers stayed in touch at first. That's how I knew about you and your brothers. Anyway, now Mother is interested in knowing how her old friend's family is doing."

"After thirty years?"

"Your mother's disappearance was a shock to her, too," Analise said as she set her uneaten sandwich back on the plate. "For years she expected Melissa to write or phone or come for a visit, but she never did."

"Yeah, well, Mom took off with another man, you know."

"Did your father ever try to find her?"

"Are you kidding? Everyone tried to find her. The police thought he'd hurt her. It was a zoo around here until she sent a postcard. She said she'd had enough, that this wasn't the life for her. Eventually I guess she made new friends and had new kids and forgot all about the old ones."

"Do you believe that?"

"Yes."

"Do your brothers?"

"Let's get one thing straight, Princess. We don't talk about my mother around here. We never have. And none of this explains why you told me you needed to be at the ranch. How much of this did you tell Cody?"

"I told him our mothers were school chums and that mine had asked me to stop here and return to Melissa's children something she'd been holding on to for years. It's a locket and it's upstairs in my room."

"And he bought that?"

"I wouldn't have come if he hadn't," she said as a flash of irritation ignited her eyes like lightning.

"Yeah, okay, point taken. But it's not really why you're here?"

"Not entirely, no."

He gestured at her plate, wishing he'd made her something fancier, a little daintier. She didn't really look like a big meat-and-potatoes kind of girl. "Maybe there's some soup left over from last night—"

She picked the sandwich up again and took a healthy bite. After chewing and swallowing, she looked him in the eye. "I'm sorry I'm beating around the bush. Isn't that the right expression?"

"Yeah, that covers it."

"The truth is my mother left something with your mother all those years ago that your mother promised to destroy. She didn't, though. Instead she wrote my mother and explained she'd decided to hide it somewhere very safe. I'm here to retrieve and destroy it."

Pierce stared at her a second before laughing. "My mother hasn't set foot on this ranch in thirty years. What in the world does your mother think you're going to be able to find after all that time?"

"I'm not at liberty to say what it is."

He opened his arms wide. "What's your plan? Search every nook and cranny? Be my guest, knock yourself out."

She narrowed her eyes. "Your mother said she had hidden this object with 'resting souls, high in the summer sky.' Does that mean something to you?"

"No," he said quickly. Okay, maybe it did bring something to mind but this was nuts. A glance out the window revealed snow coming down at a slant, meaning the storm was arriving early. Briefly, he wondered if the men had gotten the heifers back closer to the ranch.

Well, hopefully the storm would run its course by morning so these folks could depart on time. Any which way, if the one feeble clue Analise had provided pointed where Pierce thought it pointed, it was beyond reach for the time being which was fine by him.

He turned as he heard a noise at the door leading to the dining room, expecting to see someone push their way into the kitchen. Analise's gaze followed his. When no one appeared, he got off his stool and approached the door, but a sudden cry from Analise caused him to turn before he'd made it that far.

She pointed at the television with one hand and covered her mouth with the other, her beautiful eyes wide with alarm. He looked at the TV.

What appeared to be a stock photo of Analise on a ski slope filled the small flat screen. It was immediately replaced by a new photo, one of a man with a flaming red handlebar mustache. Pierce quickly adjusted the volume.

"—the driver for the daughter of King Thomas of Chatioux during her Seattle stay. Falstead's body was found stuffed into the trunk of his limousine which was pulled out of Puget Sound early this morning as commuters looked on. Police are not disclosing the cause of death at this time but sources say it appears Falstead's been dead since he was reported missing three days ago. Police plan to question Princess Analise in the days to come."

The news moved on to the next story and Pierce turned to look at Analise. She was still standing, fingertips braced on the cutting block as though they supported her entire weight.

"Your driver?"

"I didn't know his name," she said, eyelashes fluttering against pale cheeks, voice raised to be heard over the volume of the television. "I thought he didn't come that morning because he was lazy."

"Did you call the agency he worked for?"

"Personally? No, of course not. Someone must have, though."

Pierce took a step around the island. "Princess—"

"Who would do such a thing? Why?"

He shook his head. "You'd better call the Seattle Police Department."

"My mobile phone doesn't work here."

"There's one on the wall over there but the unit in the office would be more private."

"I don't know anything about Mr. Falstead," she added, but there was a resigned quality to her voice.

"Still," he said gently.

"It's my duty to check in with them. That's what you're saying. And you're right, of course. I should do it soon before they contact my father. Anyway, maybe his murder has nothing to do with…me."

He gently caught her wrist as she turned away and she looked back at him, her gaze darting to his hand. Releasing her, he added, "I think you'd be better off facing the facts."

"What facts?"

"Someone threatened you, someone killed your driver and someone injured your bodyguard. The people with the best access to you in Seattle are here right now in this house. They traveled with you."

"No," she said, but her eyes revealed she'd already grasped the truth of this statement.

At that instant, the television went dead, plunging them into tomblike silence.

They house had just lost electricity.

Chapter Six

Within minutes of the power going out, everyone had gathered in the living area, staking out real estate near the massive stone hearth in which a fire blazed. It was certainly no colder inside than it had been ten minutes before and yet they all behaved as though the temperature had taken a sudden drop.

Despite the deteriorating weather, there was ample light in the room because of the tall windows. Still, Bierta had managed to find a gloomy corner in which to stand. She'd added a bulky gray sweater to her somber uniform and held it closed with both arms wrapped around her torso. Her gaze darted from one face to the other but seemed to linger on Mr. Vaughn the longest.

Not that he seemed to notice. He stood closest to the fire, breathing on his hands, watchful in his unassuming manner.

Analise recalled the noise she and Pierce had heard at the kitchen door right before noticing the news report on the television. They'd been talking about the real reason she had insisted on coming to Wyoming.

Had one of the people in this room been on the other side of that door? Had they been eavesdropping, had they heard her mention her mother had a secret? Thank goodness she hadn't gone into details; by default, a queen's secret was a potential political landmine. Still, Analise should have made sure her bodyguard was protecting the door.

From under her eyelashes, a trick she'd perfected after spending years thwarting the paparazzi, she glanced at each face of her countrymen. Did one of them want her dead? That would mean one of them was a traitor and it was impossible to believe such a person could have hoodwinked her father's security team.

"Folks, this happens every winter, several times a winter for that matter," Pierce announced. He was not only half a head taller than anyone else in the room besides the general, he also carried himself in such a way that every head turned his direction. "It's what I was trying to warn you about when you arrived."

"You told us we had twenty-four hours," General Kaare huffed, his ramrod-straight form still encased in olive serge, ribbons and medals arranged precisely as always. Analise cast him an annoyed frown—Pierce had gone out of his way to dissuade them from staying and it was her fault they were in this situation. Surely the general realized it.

The front door burst open and as one unit they all turned to face the newcomer.

The cowhand from the airfield, the older man with the bowed legs, strode into the entry. As he continued into the living area, Toby trotted along behind.

"I bet you a buck one of them pines over in the grove dropped a branch on the power line," the older man said, addressing Pierce. "It happened a week or two ago. Power company got it fixed by the end of the day."

"The...the end of the day?" Vaughn sputtered. "But the storm—"

"There's a generator out in that building you can barely make out in this storm," Pierce said, gesturing toward a window. All Analise could see through the falling snow was a hint of green metal. "If the power isn't on by dark, we'll start it up. Anyway, by then we'll be out eating grub with the cows, right, Tex?"

Toby tipped the brim of his blue felt hat with a fingertip and tried to wink.

"I do not plan on being out in this weather," Mr. Vaughn said.

"I suggest you change your plans," Pierce said. "I want everyone where I can see them."

"Really—"

"But right now, the princess needs to use a phone. Like I explained earlier to the general, I have a couple of men detailed to keep an eye on the princess—on all of you for that matter. Can't risk any of you wandering away in the snowstorm and getting lost."

"I do not wander—" the general began, but Pierce waved him off.

"Furthermore, I want everyone to know that as far as I'm concerned the threat to Princess Analise is probably coming from one of you. When I say I'm watching, I mean it."

"This is absurd—"

"As far as you're concerned, this is my ranch and that's the way it's going down," Pierce said, once again cutting the general off. Analise noticed he didn't mention the fate of the driver. She sure as heck wasn't going to.

Without missing a beat, Pierce continued. "Jamie, you've got the only cell that gets coverage out here on a reliable basis. Call the power company on your cell and keep an eye on the boy. And where in the hell is that bodyguard?"

Jamie cleared his throat. "Last I saw he was checking out your dad's cabin."

"Oh, brother," Pierce said. "Okay, I'll take care of that next."

"What about me?" Mr. Vaughn asked.

Pierce's voice lowered to a growly, impatient tone. "Stay here and keep the fire going. The princess's maid can help you. So can the general. Firewood is accessible through the door on the hearth. Don't burn the place down."

While the general gathered himself for what would surely be another indignant protest, Bierta flung her hand toward Analise. "I will go with the princess," she said.

"Thank you, Bierta, but no," Analise said quickly. "This is a private call."

"But ma'am—"

Pierce clapped his hands together. "So, that's settled. Come with me, Princess." Analise followed him from the room. She was used to her actions being scrutinized but the way the five sets of eyes watched her now gave her the creeps. She was glad to enter the paneled room off the living area.

"The phone's over there—" Pierce began, gesturing toward the massive oak desk behind which hung a painting of a weathered wood building. Through the window on the east wall, she could see it was snowing more heavily than before.

"Do you mind if I stay while you make the call?" he asked as she walked past him.

"Don't you want to run interference between your father and my bodyguard?"

"It can wait a minute."

"I don't mind," she told him. The truth was she was spooked and she welcomed his presence.

The call took several minutes to go through. Once connected with the right office, she found the detective she needed to talk to was unavailable. Assured he would call back the next day, Analise left the ranch number and glanced across the room at Pierce.

He was staring at her, his gray eyes intense. As she opened her mouth to explain the call, he spoke.

"Who are you going to marry?"

Not what she expected. "His name is Ricard Molinaix."

"Successful?"

"Yes, very."

Pierce turned to look out the window. "You've been faithful to him?"

"I don't see—"

He turned around, holding up both hands. "I'm just trying to make sense of all this."

"Ricard would never go to such extremes for any reason, least of all me."

He cocked an eyebrow. "You are exactly the kind of woman that pushes a man to extremes. Beautiful, rich—"

"Don't waste your time worrying about Ricard."

"Remember how I told you about watching someone when they speak?"

"Yes."

"I watched you tell me about your mother's lost belongings. There's something you're not telling me."

"Well, of course there is. I can't disclose the exact nature of the… items. Not just because of you, but because of the possibility someone might overhear me talking about it."

"Like someone did when we were in the kitchen," he stated bluntly.

"Yes. Like that."

"The eavesdropper might have been anyone and that anyone might have been innocent. Maybe they paused because they heard voices in conversation and didn't want to interrupt."

"Maybe," she agreed. "But given everything, I don't think so."

"I don't, either. And you can't think of anyone who wants to harm you except for a political faction back in Chatioux who is using threats against you to control your father?"

"That's correct."

He put out a hand. "All right then. I think it's time to find out what's going on with your bodyguard. Get your coat. You're coming with me."

As she left to find out what Bierta had done with her jacket, she saw Pierce work the combination on the locked gun cabinet. He was withdrawing a handgun as she left the room.

BRAD HARLEY, THE bodyguard, was standing outside the house under the front portico, smoking a cigarette, sunglasses firmly in place. He slipped something silver into his pocket—a gun. Analise wasn't fond of guns, but seeing the bodyguard take his job seriously reassured her.

"None of the princess's party is to go in or out of the house except the kid," Pierce said briskly. "And don't leave this post, okay?"

With thumb and forefinger, Harley pulled the cigarette from between his lips. "I don't take orders from you," he said as he blew smoke.

Analise cleared her throat. "Do as he says, Mr. Harley."

The two men glared at one another until Pierce led the way around the covered decks and down a short flight of stairs. They hurried through the snow until climbing another flight of stairs, this one leading to a smaller log structure. Analise was glad for Pierce's steadying hand on her elbow as the freezing snow made footing treacherous.

The housekeeper opened the door before they could knock and stepped outside, Bonnie close on her heels. The dog nuzzled Analise's hand before dashing off through the snow to the barn. Pauline closed the door behind her.

"Power out in the main house, too? I was just coming back to the house to check the stew. Good thing the new stove uses gas."

"Jamie's calling the electric company," Pierce told her. "On another subject, do you know if the princess's bodyguard talked to my father?"

"He came by but I wouldn't let him in. He said he had to know exactly who's on the ranch. Like anyone knows that what with all the people coming and going. I told him to stay away." With a quick but reverent glance at Analise, she added, "Hope that's okay, Your Highness."

"It's fine."

"We need to see Dad," Pierce said.

The housekeeper's gaze strayed to Analise then flashed back to Pierce. "Are you sure that's wise?"

"No," Pierce said. "But it's a safe place for her to be right now and that's what matters."

"Safe? What do you mean?"

"She's in danger," he said, trying to hurry this little talk along and get out of the cold.

"In danger?" Pauline repeated, looking over their shoulders at the near blizzard raging behind them. "From what?"

"We're not sure, but it's a *who,* not a *what.*"

"Wait a moment," Analise said. "Is that why you brought me out here? I don't need someone to watch over me."

He pinned her with his gray eyes. "The hell you don't. I'm not leaving you alone in that house with those people, not after what we heard and saw—you know what I mean. Anyway, Pauline has things to do for the cookout and Dad gets lonely. You'll see. It'll be great." He ruined this by adding, "Just don't mention my mother to him."

"Pierce—"

"What does *she* know about your mother?" Pauline snapped as she bunched the collar of her coat at her throat. She darted a glance at Analise. The sudden change in her voice and manner was alarming.

"My mother went to school with Pierce's mother," Analise was quick to say.

"It's no big deal," Pierce added. "You know how Dad is."

Pauline's compressed lips announced she wasn't entirely sure she believed either one of them, which aroused Analise's curiosity. Was it possible this woman was jealous of Melissa Browning? Had she even met Melissa or had she come here after Melissa left?

"I'd better stay—"

"What I would appreciate you doing," Pierce

interrupted, "is going back inside the house and seeing to the rest of our guests."

Pauline stared hard at Pierce for a moment and then nodded curtly. "Don't you upset him," she scolded softly. "I know how you two are with each other."

Pierce held the door open and Analise scooted inside the overheated cabin, glad to get out of the cold. She understood why Pierce was parking her out here away from the others, but did he have to be so high handed about it?

THIS WAS EITHER a really smart move or a really dumb one. Pierce wasn't sure which, just that the thought of leaving Analise alone with Vaughn and Kaare and that creepy maid was more than he could bring himself to do. He couldn't drag her out to the barn and around, not dressed as she was in silk and diamonds, so that left plan B—his father.

The cabin had been built years before as guest quarters, back in the days when Pierce's mother had still been on the ranch. She'd loved to throw parties and many times, because of the ranch's remote location, the guests had stayed overnight.

Until his father hurt himself, Adam had lived in the cabin alone, but its single-story construction meant it was easier for Birch to manage during his recovery so he'd moved in, too. Adam had recently started his own place closer to the lake though Pierce had only seen it from a distance.

He found his father in front of the largest window in the place, seated in a wheelchair with a cast on his leg. Due to closed drapes, the room was dark except for the flickering fire in the grate and pool of light that surrounded the old man thanks to a kerosene lamp burning atop a wooden table at his side.

The closed drapes surprised—and alarmed—Pierce. His father wasn't the kind to sit inside and let the ranch work around him. Even injured, he kept a hand in the day-to-day business of running the place or at least he had before. This development was a surprise to Pierce and he suspected concern for their father was why Cody had really asked Pierce to drop everything and come home.

Birch Westin wore his steel-gray hair long and combed back from his high forehead. He had always been a big, gruff man's man, larger than life, so sure of himself he seldom suffered a moment's hesitation, and his looks reflected it. In the past, he'd been a man as brown as sun-scorched grass in late August, skin deeply etched by the unrelenting elements with a stride that covered ground like a Mack truck on a runaway hill.

But this year he'd been out of commission

thanks to the busted patella which was now held together with pins and wire, plus he'd suffered two post-operative infections. That meant indoor time, hence a paler complexion. Pierce wasn't sure if it was the change in his coloring or the weeks of illness, but his dad looked frail sitting there.

"Who's that with you?" Birch asked, closing the book that had been open on his lap.

"This is Ms. Emille," Pierce said, suspecting his father was about as likely to recognize Princess Analise's face or name as he was that of a rock star. Hopefully Analise wouldn't mind he'd dropped her title from the introduction. "Ms. Emille, Birch Westin."

She held out a hand and his father stared at it. "How in the world did you get here in this storm?"

"We came before the storm, by helicopter, sir," she replied as her hand drifted back to her side. "And, please, call me Analise."

"Helicopter?"

"She and her friends needed a place to wait out the storm," Pierce said. "The pilot saw the ranch and landed. I was hoping you'd entertain her while I go out to the barn."

"How many of 'em?"

"How many of them what?"

A narrowing of the steely eyes. "How many

friggin' people are parading around the ranch in this storm? I thought I heard a kid whooping it up a while ago and someone knocked at the door but Pauline sent them away."

"Six in all," Analise volunteered. "I'm sorry if we've bothered you."

"You haven't bothered me," he said, flicking her a glance. When he frowned the way he was right now, his lips all but disappeared. Pierce swallowed a sharp retort and added, "They'll be gone tomorrow."

"The Open Sky is no place for visitors. You should know that. Guess you forgot what real work is like. 'Course, Cody or Adam would have known how to get rid of them."

"No doubt," Pierce said, hoping the princess had the sense not to take his father's comments personally.

Birch finally shook his head. "She can sit over there. Won't bother me."

"I can stoke the fire for you," Analise said, moving in front of the rock hearth. Firelight bathed the blue blackness of her hair, flickered over her flawless features as she threw a glance over her shoulder at Pierce. Suddenly ambushed by the desire to touch her, Pierce looked away. Why couldn't the two of them be alone in this storm, in this room? Why did she have to be a damn princess?

"It's too dark in here for you to mess with the fire," Birch snarled and as though on command, the lights flickered back on and the room was suddenly way too bright.

Pierce caught sight of the shotgun resting near his father's feet. "I see you're armed and loaded. Just don't shoot the—er, Ms. Emille, okay?"

"You must have something better to do than stand in here yammering at me," Birch snapped, and with that, the book flew open again and he buried his nose in the pages.

Pierce stared down at him, frustrated by the old man's habitual belligerence. For his dad, nothing had changed since Pierce was an eighteen-year-old screw-up who was in trouble more than he was out of it. There could be no redemption because Pierce wasn't willing to pay the price.

Truth: he wasn't even sure what the price was.

With an apologetic glance at Analise, he turned on his heels and left.

Chapter Seven

With the trees cleared from the power line, the electricity up and running and Analise surviving his father, afternoon drifted into evening in a nice, unhurried way.

"Your people did a great job," Analise said.

They were standing in the pavilion where a huge fire roared in the center fire pit. Somehow Jamie and the hands had rounded up a few cows and convinced them to stay nearby while someone else had actually used the tractor to haul the old covered wagon out of storage and set it up under the roof. It was missing a wheel or two and sat at a rakish angle and the cloth was torn and stained, but so what? It gave the place a lot of atmosphere.

Jamie perched on a bale of hay playing old songs on his harmonica while another longtime hand performed lasso tricks and a woman everyone called Sassy Sally made a big deal of heating a branding iron. Every once in a while, she'd pull it out of the coals and burn the Open Sky Ranch logo, an intertwined impression of OSR, into a piece of wood while Toby watched with great, huge eyes. Bonnie lay curled in the straw that was an almost exact match to her fur.

Pots of bubbling food and smoke from grilling gave the air a pungent smell. Well, that and the cows and horses and the straw, some still in bales, some strewn around on the floor. All and all, with the night hovering around the perimeter and snowflakes revealed by the ambient light right out of reach, it made a cozy, if somewhat breezy, place to spend the evening.

And Analise looked amazing. She'd produced a white Stetson with a feather headband and she wore it like a tiara on her dark hair. Her perfect-fitting jeans were now tucked into what appeared to be handmade ostrich Western-style boots.

Must be nice to be rolling in dough.

"Is something wrong?" she asked him.

"Was I staring at you?"

She sat down on one of the bales. "Yes."

He sat down beside her, unable to tear his gaze from her face. "Sorry. You're just so damn over-the-top."

"What does that mean?" she asked, brows furrowing together.

"It means you're gorgeous."

"You think I'm gorgeous?" she asked, and he laughed at her innocent expression.

"Yes, Princess, you're gorgeous. I guess you hear that a lot."

She cocked her head and floated an eyebrow under the brim of her hat. "Now, why would I hear that a lot?"

"Don't the people around you say stuff like that?"

"Not on a regular basis, no."

"How about Ricard?"

"Why are you so interested in Ricard?" she asked, meeting his gaze.

"You know why."

"No—"

"Yes, you do. How about your posse? They must be full of compliments."

"My posse?"

He nodded in the general direction of the rest of her crew. He'd spent the afternoon telling every man or woman on the ranch to keep an eye on this band of no-goods, but they weren't prisoners and so he had no way to demand they all stay in one spot where they'd be easy to track. Right now he could see Vaughn over by the chuck wagon talking to Pauline, his foot keeping time to the music; the maid sitting by herself on a bale of straw looking miserable and out of sorts. Kaare was nowhere in sight.

Pierce looked around for Darrell Cox, the man Lucas Garvey had enlisted to help him act as an unofficial bodyguard for the princess. He'd seen Darrell an hour or two before, decked out in a bright blue kerchief knotted around his huge neck, keeping an eagle eye, but right this moment he was missing. Garvey was standing close to the cows, though he seemed as mesmerized by the princess as the other men whose gazes darted to her over and over.

"General Kaare cares about my position, not me," the princess said in what he was beginning to understand was her frank and unpretentious way of looking at her world. "Mr. Vaughn is something of a zealot. Bierta is afraid of me for no good reason. The bodyguard—where is Mr. Harley, anyway?"

Pierce looked around. They were some distance from the house and for the first time, he realized he couldn't see any lights coming from that direction. As the pavilion was lit only by lantern and firelight, he wasn't sure when the electricity had gone out again.

"If I were you, I'd fire that guy," Pierce said as he stood, but a far more ominous reason to be concerned about him crossed his mind. He was the hired replacement for the injured bodyguard from Chatioux, hired by whom? Pierce made a mental note to find out. For now, he needed to get the generator up and running. Wouldn't do to have these people ferried back to the house only to be shown to their rooms with flashlights.

She touched his hand as she stood beside him. "What about my mother's request? I know other things have happened that may make this seem trivial to you, but it's not. Have you thought any more about it?"

He looked down at her anxious face, her blue eyes piercing him, and wished he could hand her what she wanted. "I might know the place she's talking about, Princess, but there's no way we can get there now. The storm made that impossible."

"But by tomorrow—"

"Maybe," he said, resisting the urge to take her hand. At the moment she looked so earnest and so young and so vulnerable, it aroused every protective bone in his body and he had to admit that was annoying. He'd given that up years before when Patrick died and Erin left. Now he used his protective instincts to safeguard his business, not loved ones.

Well, in a way, the princess was a business, right? The ranch sure as hell was a business and right now, his to take care of. He felt better. "Let's see what happens," he told her. "It's up to the weather."

"Then I'll pray the weather gods are smiling down on us."

"It's that important to you?"

"It's that important, *period*." He followed her gaze to her cousin who had drooped onto a bale of hay, eyes half-closed, toy gun dangling from weary fingers. Talk about innocent and vulnerable, and yet again a knot formed in his throat.

"I think Tex is about done in," she said. "So am I, for that matter."

He was loath to have her out of his sight.

Once again he looked around for her bodyguard or Lucas Garvey or Darrell Cox and saw none of them. Things were definitely winding down, though. Ranch hands were beginning to clear tables and lead livestock away, the music had stopped, the fire was dying down. "We'll send Toby back with Pauline and Mr. Vaughn and the maid. It's hard to tell for sure but it sure looks like the power went out again. Where's the general?"

"I don't know."

"I would appreciate it if you'd stay with me until I can personally lock you in your room."

Her gaze darted every direction, fear creeping into her eyes. "I don't know if that's necessary."

"We could see if Dad is still awake if you'd prefer."

"I think once today was enough for him," she muttered.

"Probably."

While she convinced her maid to go on without her, Pierce arranged transportation with Pauline and sent someone off to look for the general. He found Lucas Garvey drinking coffee by the covered wagon, back behind the tattered cloth. He was obviously taking his job as bodyguard seriously, for Pierce noticed a gun holstered on his hip.

"Have you seen the man called Harley? He's the official bodyguard with this party."

Lucas shook his head. "Not for a while."

"Where was he when you last saw him?"

Lucas threw the last of his coffee onto the straw-covered ground and set the tin cup aside. "It was an hour or so ago. He was standing near the barn talking to Darrell."

Pierce hooked his hands on his waist, looked around at the departing guests and the waiting princess and sighed. "Okay, you find Harley and tell him to hightail it to the house and do what he was hired to do. Then you come along and bring Darrell if you can find him quickly."

He and the princess took off through the snow to the outbuilding where the generator was housed, holding their hats on their heads against the wind. The storm had abated some but it was still slow slogging their way through the elements.

Using the wavering beam from the flashlight, Pierce slid the wooden door open and they stepped in out of the worst of the weather. He closed the door behind them. The light played over the generator as they stepped inside. It was the same old gasoline model that had been out here for twenty or thirty years. Melted snow on the cement floor suggested someone had been there before them. Pierce checked the gas gauge, relieved to see it had fuel, but why hadn't it started? As Analise stood close by shivering, he switched it on and pulled the choke, then yanked the cord.

Nothing.

"Is something wrong?" she asked.

"I don't know," he said, noticing the batteries in his flashlight were running low. The light was wavering and growing weak. He handed it to Analise. "Look around and see if there's a lantern on the bench over there. Dad used to keep two or three out here for emergencies. I don't need to see this thing to pull the cord."

She took the light and moved off toward the bench as Pierce once again put some muscle into the job. He was in the middle of another attempt when Analise screamed and dropped the flashlight. With a crack, it hit the cement floor and went out. The room went from shadowed to pitch-black.

A small sob filled the darkness.

Chapter Eight

"Princess!"

Analise stood stock-still, afraid to move, shaking so hard her teeth rattled.

Maybe the man wasn't dead. She had to check.

Even as she knelt, she knew there was no point. She'd seen the horrible bulging of his eyes, the purple tongue. Even now his open eyes seemed to stare through the cold black air right into hers....

"Princess Analise, answer me. Are you okay?"

"I'm okay," she whispered, but it carried in the still air like a shout. Her knees hit the floor and she put out her hands, searching for the flashlight, jumping when she felt cold flesh instead.

"Stay where you are. I'll find you," Pierce said. She was vaguely aware of the sound of him moving toward her. A moment later, his voice was closer. "Are you hurt?"

"It's not me," she said. "It's a man. I—I think he's dead."

Pierce knelt beside her, directed by her voice perhaps, his shoulder bumping into hers, his hand closing on her arm.

"Who?"

"I don't know. I think he was strangled."

She felt Pierce moving beside her, his hands searching the floor in front of them just as she had. A grunt disclosed he'd found something. She stopped breathing. The next thing she knew, he'd stood up and pulled her to her feet.

Wrapping his arms around her, their hats bumping together, he spoke softly into her ear. "I don't know who it is, but you're right, he's dead."

"Oh my God," she said through chattering teeth. "I—I thought I saw something twisted in a blue scarf."

"Did you say the scarf was blue?"

"Yes." She swallowed a sob as the next words tumbled out. "It clashed with his face."

"Blue," he repeated, then his grip on her tightened.

"Do you know who it is?" she asked, voice trembling.

"I think so."

"I'm sorry," she whispered against his neck.

"Sorry? About what?"

"I've never seen a dead man before. I mean

on television, yes, but not for real. I shouldn't be trembling. This isn't about me."

"Shh," he said softly. "You have nothing to be sorry for. Listen, Princess, there isn't anywhere in this building for a killer to hide, but there's forty feet between us and the house, and if someone wants to ambush us there's not a lot to stop him except my Smith & Wesson. Stay behind me, okay?"

He opened the door and they waited for a second, listening. The wind rattled a window somewhere, sent tree limbs scratching against metal somewhere else. The falling snow was barely visible. The world was a dark place, a secret place.

They moved slowly, fumbling their way in the dark, holding hands so they wouldn't get separated, the snow up to their knees in places. The forty feet took forever to cross. The steps to the house rose out of nowhere and they stumbled up them. Pierce pulled her into the deepest shadows of the porch as they circled the house. "We'll go in the kitchen door," he whispered.

Soft, flickering light showed through the kitchen windows now that they were almost on top of them and they found the door with little trouble. Pierce pulled it open quickly and they catapulted inside what appeared to be an anteroom to the kitchen, heaving, covered with snow.

He clicked the dead bolt and quickly pulled the curtain across the window. It all happened in a blur.

They burst into the kitchen a second later. Pauline backed up to the sink, candles in her hands. "What the blazes?" she cried as Bonnie jumped to her feet, her growl turning to a tail wag in the blink of an eye.

"Keep the doors locked," Pierce commanded. "Don't open them. I'll explain in a minute. Do you have a flashlight we can use?"

"I sent them all upstairs with the princess's party," Pauline said, her gaze flicking over Analise. "My dear, are you all right? You're pale as a ghost."

Analise didn't trust herself to speak, but the soft feel of the Lab's warm body pressed against her leg was oddly comforting. After the nightmare of the past few minutes, it was a shock to find the house so quiet and warm and normal.

Pauline plucked an electric lantern off the counter and handed it to Pierce. "Take this. I've got lots of candles down here. What's going on, Pierce? Why didn't you start the generator?"

"There's been an accident in the shed," Pierce said softly. "I think it's Darrell Cox."

Her eyes widened. "I'll go—"

"No! Stay inside. Lock the doors. I'll see the princess to her room and then be back. Trust me, there's nothing we can do for whoever is out there, not now."

"It wasn't an accident, was it? That's why you want me to lock the doors. Oh, poor Darrell. He and the Lindquist girl just announced their engagement."

"Have you seen Lucas Garvey or the princess's bodyguard?" Pierce asked Pauline.

"Not for a long time."

"Keep Bonnie with you, okay?"

There were more candles on the dining room table and spaced throughout the house leading toward the stairs. They moved quickly.

"Where will your maid sleep?" Pierce asked Analise as they reached the stairs.

"In my room. There's a day bed as well as a queen—"

"And Toby?" he interrupted.

"He has the room next door to mine."

"There are twin beds in that room," he said at the same time he opened the door to Analise's room. It, too, was bathed in soft light, this from two kerosene lanterns. Bierta, wrapped in a dark green robe, was in the process of laying Analise's nightgown on the bed. She looked up at them, her face a pale oval.

"Come with us," Pierce said.

"But—"

"Just come," Analise coaxed though she had no idea what he had in mind.

Bierta paused for a second before dutifully following them from the room. Using the flashlight, Pierce led them the short distance down the hall to the next door and opened it. An electric lantern like the one Pauline had given to Birch sat atop the dresser and revealed the still form of a child asleep in the bed closest to the window. Toby's red hair was all that showed of him. Pierce urged Bierta inside. "Quiet, don't wake the boy."

"But the princess," Bierta protested, eyes beseeching Analise. "Your Highness, please, I'm frightened, I don't understand—"

"I'll explain everything in a minute," Analise promised with a gentle touch on her maid's arm. *Explain this? How?*

Pierce closed the door and faced Analise, towering over her, the tension in his handsome face visible despite the spotty lighting. "Take this," he said, pressing the revolver into her hands. "Sit at the desk in there and point that gun at anything that moves. If your maid sneezes, shoot her."

"And **shall** I shoot Toby if he rolls over?" she snapped and was immediately sorry she had. It wasn't Pierce's fault all this was happening—it was hers.

But his eyes softened as he peered down at her and the ghost of a smile played across his lips. "I'll leave that to your judgment. Don't open this door until you hear my voice. You know what I sound like, right?"

"I know what you sound like. You're going back out to the shed to see to that poor man?"

The accumulated snow on his hat had begun to melt and dripped onto his broad shoulders. "I have to make sure it's Darrell and that he's really beyond help."

The door next to Toby's opened and a light blinded them for an instant. Pierce turned his light in that direction and illuminated General Kaare, still dressed in his uniform. His expression went from annoyed to alarmed as he studied Analise and Pierce. "What is going on? Is this man bothering you, Princess Analise?"

"No. Please, just go to bed."

He turned cold black eyes on Pierce. "What about the power? Didn't you say something about a generator?"

"There'll be no power tonight. Where is Vaughn and where is that worthless bodyguard?"

The door across the hall opened. Dressed in a muted red dressing gown, Vaughn stood framed in the doorway. One look at the gun in Analise's hands and he retreated inside and slammed the door.

"Mr. Vaughn abhors violence," the princess said.

"I don't know where Harley is," Kaare added.

"Then do what the princess asked and keep your nose out of this."

"Princess, allow me to help you. Give me the weapon. We will adjourn to your room."

"She doesn't need you protecting her," Pierce said. "And as for her room, I'll stay in there with her tonight."

The general's eyes all but bugged out of his head. "I protest—"

"Call your embassy, but that's what's going down. I don't trust any of you. The maid and boy will sleep in this room. When I get back from… an errand, I'll bunk in with the princess, you'll stay in your room and Mr. Vaughn will stay in his."

"Princess, really. You cannot condone—"

"I think it sounds like a good plan," Analise said quickly.

"Where is Harley? We're paying him good money to see to your safety."

"No one seems to know where he is. I'm beginning to wonder *what* he is."

Pierce opened Toby's door and lowering his voice, repeated himself to Analise. "Go inside, Princess. Lock the door. Don't open it for anyone but me."

"This is outrageous," Kaare grumbled.

"You don't know the half of it," Pierce muttered as he gently pushed Analise inside. She leaned back against the closed door. She should have told Pierce to be careful.

"Your...Your Highness?" Bierta whispered.

For now there was Bierta to reassure.

SOMEONE HAD FASHIONED a garrote by twisting a wooden stick through Darrell's blue kerchief and applying pressure.

Pierce shook his head at the terrible loss of life that lay before him, swerving his light away, sad to the bones. The kid couldn't be over twenty.

He illuminated the generator. For the first time he noticed a puddle on the floor beneath the gas tank and a half-empty water bottle lying on its side. Had someone stuck water in the tank? That would mean the machine was sabotaged. Was that how the murderer coaxed Darrell into this building? Had they convinced him to try to start the generator and then when he was busy, stuck that stick into the blue kerchief and twisted? If so, it meant a smaller man than Darrell could have killed him.

A sound at the door sent Pierce twisting quickly. He'd taken a shotgun from the gun cabinet before returning to the shed and that now found its way into both hands.

"Damn, don't shoot," Lucas Garvey shouted, both hands in the air, his own flashlight in the snow where he'd apparently just dropped it. "I was just coming to tell you I can't find Darrell. No one's seen him for a couple of hours. The bodyguard is dead drunk out behind the barn. I got a couple of guys to help me get him bedded down in a stall to sleep it off so he don't freeze to death out there."

Pierce suspected that was about as much talking as any Garvey man had ever done. He said, "Listen to me, Lucas. Forget the bodyguard. Darrell has been murdered. He's in here." As he spoke, he came outside, hooked a lock through the hasp and twisted the dial.

"Darrell is dead?" Lucas said, staring at the door.

"Yeah. I'm sorry. I guess you guys were pals."

Lucas rubbed one of his thin cheeks as he picked up the flashlight he'd dropped.

"Don't tell anyone else for now," Pierce cautioned.

"Should I report this to the boss?"

"You mean my father? Lord, no. Let him sleep. Go check on the bodyguard, make sure he's just drunk, okay? Then get some sleep. I've got to go call the police."

And get Analise back into her room, he added to himself. *Away from all of them, safe behind a locked door...with me.*

Chapter Nine

Back in her own bathroom, Analise discovered
the only nightwear Bierta had packed for her was
skimpy, flesh-colored silk and it clung to every
curve with a single-minded tenacity that Analise
had never before noticed. Hardly the right thing
to wear in front of a stranger.

As she cinched the matching robe tight around
her waist and hoped for the best, she was glad
for the power outage. Her lips lifted into a wry
smile as she acknowledged to herself that Pierce
was right about one thing—the paparazzi would
love to be privy to this situation. Princess Caught
with Cowboy in Middle of Murder Mayhem!

How terrible that such violence should visit
such a spot, and even worse because she suspected she'd brought it with her.

It had to be the bodyguard, Harley. It couldn't
be Bierta or Vaughn or even General Kaare. She
closed her eyes for a second and tried to remember if any of them had left the pavilion that eve-

ning, but the truth was she'd been so caught up in Toby's excitement and her own budding awareness of Pierce Westin that she hadn't noticed. For a while, it had seemed like the last few days of threats and fear had been a bad dream.

When she reentered the bedroom, she found Pierce standing at the vanity. He looked up as she entered, a diamond tiara in his hand. "You travel with two of these things?" he asked.

"Don't even ask," she said. "There's a ball gown in the closet, too."

He flashed a weak smile as he carefully put the tiara back in its open case. He crossed to the small bed that had been intended for Bierta and sat down. What a smile he had. What a face. Even the dark haze of a growing beard looked good on him, defining his jawline, and though his clothes were casual, he wore them with such assurance he might have been born in them.

In a way he was. Funny how hard it was to remember he didn't live or work here anymore. She knew when she thought of him in the future, it would always be in connection with this ranch.

"Where did you acquire the tan?" she asked as she sat next to him. He'd already informed her the dead man was indeed his employee Darrell Cox. And just for a little while she wanted to talk about something else.

"I was in Naples, Italy, less than a week ago," he said, his voice as soft as falling snow.

The image of Naples filled her with light. "Oh, I love it there."

"When were you there?"

"Several times over the years. My grandparents' palazzo overlooked Naples Bay. My brother and I spent summers with them when we were children."

"That must have been nice. Just getting away from being royal must have been a relief for a kid."

"Well, actually, Grandmother was a king's daughter, just as I am, and Grandfather was a duke."

"Man, it's the family business, isn't it? Do you guys get group discounts on crown jewels?"

She smiled. "Very funny. What were you doing in Naples?"

He sat up straighter. "That's where our latest job is. We've been more or less on the road for the past five years."

"On the road?"

"Moving from job to job."

"Doesn't that get tiresome?"

"Hell, no, I like it. My partner is making noise about selling out but that's just because his girlfriend wants to get married."

"And you don't think much of marriage," she said.

He shrugged. "I used to."

"What happened to yours?"

He turned slightly to face her and his voice grew incredibly soft. "We had a little boy. Patrick. He was my whole world. After he died, my wife and I drifted apart. I threw myself into work, she needed things I didn't know how to give her. But the truth is, I don't think the marriage would have lasted anyway. She came from a home with so many stepparents she'd lost count and I came from this place."

"This doesn't seem like such a bad place to come from," she said.

"You've met my father."

"I am used to men like your father. They often have soft insides."

For a second, Pierce's gaze delved very deep into her eyes, and then he shook his head. "I don't think he was always so abrupt. I've heard he adored my mother. She was a socialite, way, way out of his league in so many ways. Why in the world a woman like her thought marrying a confirmed cowboy would lead to happiness is a mystery. Her leaving like she did, running off with another man, well, it undid him. He wasn't the same, or at least that's what Jamie says. It changed him."

"And it affected all of her sons."

"Yeah. Well, Cody was the oldest. He's the one who remembers her best. He married a woman very much like her. I think from the moment he brought her here he was waiting for her to leave and sure enough, she did a couple years later. Adam barely remembers Mom and wants nothing to do with her."

"He's the one who wants a nice farm girl?"

"Yes. Someone who understands what the ranching life is really about. A woman from the same background, someone down-to-earth. Adam has great plans for this place and the herd."

"That seems very reasonable to me."

"I suppose."

"And what was your wife like?"

He grinned. "Erin was a lot like me. Wild. Crazy. Didn't believe in much of anything, in and out of trouble as a kid, just like I was. I married her within a few months of leaving here. Then I joined the army and that straightened me out. It also kept me away from home for months at a time so Erin did her thing while I did mine and the marriage seemed good. She got pregnant when I finally left the army. Maybe our son would have helped her get her head on straight, I don't know. We only had a year with him, too little time to tell. After she left, my old army buddy talked me into going into business with him and now you know the whole Pierce Westin story."

"Do you miss the ranch? There have been generations of Westins here, right? Isn't it in your blood, too?"

He shrugged. "Kind of. I can't deny being back here has been good in a way. Calving season is about to begin, then there will be driving the cows to the high pastures for summer—it's really beautiful up there, you'd love it. Then there's haying and branding and finally market day followed by another long winter—it all starts over again. There's a hardworking rhythm to it that you don't find everywhere. It gets into you."

He looked at her and produced a half smile. "But that was a lifetime ago. Before my marriage, before Patrick's short life or my new career, a long time ago."

"I can't imagine what it was like for you and your wife to lose your baby," she said softly. "I'm very sorry." What would it be like to lose a child? How could anyone ever take a chance like that again, and yet how could they not? If you lost a child and were afraid to try again, didn't that mean you lived in shadows, caught in the past?

She wanted to ask him more questions but hesitated. She'd be gone tomorrow and the false sense of intimacy between them was already hard to cope with.

It was false, wasn't it? People didn't really connect this fast....

"For a long time it took courage just to wake up in the morning," he said. "But they say time heals all wounds."

"Do you believe that?"

He shook his head. "No, but it kind of wears away the sharp edges." After a second, he added, "Your turn. Tell me what Ricard is like."

She glanced at him, but there was just curiosity in his eyes. "Our fathers were childhood friends. Ricard and I have known each other forever although he's almost a decade older than I am."

"Royal?"

"Titled."

"Appropriate mate for a princess?"

"Yes."

"What's he look like?"

She smiled at his questions. "Good-looking in his own way. He's a businessman, very polished."

"Do you love him?"

"No."

"Does he love you?"

She smiled. "No. Well, maybe I'm being unfair. Do we love each other? Yes. Are we in love with each other? No."

"Maybe that's better than the other way around," he said. "Is he rich?"

She shrugged. "His family is very prominent and yes, he's wealthy. Above all, he has an important future within his family and desires a son of his own to pass it on to. Our backgrounds are similar, our families friendly. There should be no major roadblocks."

"And that means a lot to you?"

"Of course."

"But it's not very interesting."

Her shoulders lifted in a shrug and she stared at her hands. "It's expected."

He touched her chin and raised her face to his, dropping his hand at once. "I kind of hate to admit I think this way, Princess, but that's not good enough for you."

"Why don't you call me Analise?"

"I'm not sure. Just seems smarter to keep things a little formal, I guess."

"I'd like to hear you say my name."

He smiled. "Okay, Princess Analise. There you go."

She pushed on his shoulder and he caught her hand. Her breath caught as he lowered and held it against his chest. The strong thrumming of his heart resonated in her fingertips.

The heat of his body seemed to swell between them, to envelop her. His grasp was tender but firm, his breathing steady. And his mouth was agonizingly close...

She leaned forward and kissed him.

His lips felt like velvet.

In the next instant she drew away, but his hand had slipped around to the back of her neck, tangled in her hair, and getting away wasn't so easy. Besides, she didn't want to get away, not really.

What?

What was she thinking?

His mouth was warm and wet, enticing, captivating, his kisses so deep they seemed forged from years of desire. And desire was exactly what they aroused. Hot, burning—

She jerked away, stunned as much by her thoughts as by her behavior. "I'm—I'm sorry," she stammered.

"Really?"

"No. Yes."

His smile looked wistful. "I didn't think they made women like you anymore, Princess."

"You're making fun of me," she said, but at the same time, every inch of her body tingled. She suddenly wanted to do all those wild things she'd spent years denying.

"I just thought the modern woman was as open to sexual gratification as any man."

"I have obligations that preclude being free to do whatever I want, whenever I want." It was a lecture she'd given herself any number of times, but now the words sounded hollow. "I know it's old-fashioned," she added miserably.

"But it suits you. And there can never be anything between us."

"No, there can't."

"Because you're a princess."

"That's not why. This isn't the Dark Age."

"Then why?"

She shook her head and looked away.

"Come on, spill your guts. Tell me what you're thinking."

"We're too different," she said.

"Haven't you heard that opposites attract?"

"I'm not talking about attraction," she said softly.

"Ah. Okay, I get your point."

"Kissing you was selfish indulgence on my part."

"Indulge yourself any time you wish," he said. He released her hand as he stood. For a long moment he stared down at her, his face only half-visible. "I think it's a good idea to get a little shut-eye, don't you?"

"I am tired," she admitted.

But he didn't turn away. Instead, he pulled her to her feet and studied her face. "You have your Ricard," he said at last. "You have your chance for everything you want."

What she wanted was standing nine inches in front of her. Why didn't he just fling her down on the bed and take her? Or better yet, go away? One or the other.

Wait a second. How incredibly selfish could one person be? A man had died here tonight. He'd been killed and another before him in Seattle, and she was worried about her love life? Thoroughly ashamed, she added, "Did you know Darrell well?"

"I'd never met him before this afternoon."

"Your housekeeper said he was engaged." Her throat closed on the last word. All the promise that word encompassed, all the hope and the joy...

He touched her chin and she raised her gaze to his. "What is it, Princess?"

"He wouldn't be dead if I hadn't come here."

"And you wouldn't have come here if your mother hadn't given my mother something to destroy that my mother hid instead. Is Darrell's murder their fault?"

"Of course not."

"And it's not yours, either. Listen, what's important now is Darrell was one of two men I assigned to keep a close eye on you. The bodyguard you hired in Seattle is passed out in the barn. The other man I asked to stay sharp found him outside in the snow drunker than a skunk."

"Drunk!"

"Did the Seattle cops call you back?"

"No. Did you call local authorities about Darrell?"

"Yes. They told me to secure the murder scene which I'd already done and promised to come out here as soon as the weather clears. For now it's just us. And no one can leave until they've questioned all of you."

She shook her head. "I'll have to call my father and inform him what's happened. I can't allow him to be dissuaded from doing what is right for Chatioux because I might be in danger."

"Do you want to call now?"

Her smile was fleeting. "No, it's early morning there, not the best time to reach him. I'll get some sleep and call later."

"Okay. One more thing. Who hired this bodyguard?"

"The general."

"So Vaughn drives you into a trap and the general hires the bodyguard that turns out to be a drunk?"

"It looks that way. Maybe that's why Mr. Harley wore sunglasses all the time."

"To hide bloodshot eyes? Maybe." He sighed deeply and her heart went out to him. It was true he dealt with lawbreakers, but she doubted he was any more accustomed to seeing a man choked to death than she was. And he'd had to go look a second time....

"I just want to get you off this ranch and back to Chatioux in one piece," he said. "You have to be careful, Princess. Trust no one. Promise me."

"Not even you?"

"You can trust me. I know my place. You're safe with me."

"That's not what I meant," she said, amazed at how much had happened between them in so short a time.

His fingers quickly grazed her cheek. "I know. Get some sleep."

SOMETIME DURING THE night she awoke with a start, heart hammering. She'd been in Chatioux, in her room. There'd been a knocking sound. She'd walked through the castle, through the endless corridors, up flights of winding stairs, around turrets and down through dungeons, looking for the cause of the knocking as it grew louder and louder until she'd found a pine casket on a stone floor. Horrified, she'd realized the sound came from inside the casket. And when she'd lifted the lid, she'd found her own lifeless face staring back at her.

Now she sat up as she finally realized there was someone knocking softly at the bedroom door.

Pierce got out of the chair near the window

and moved silently to the door. "Who is it?" he asked in a very low voice.

The response sounded agitated. "It's Lucas."

Pierce opened the door, his form visible in the light cast by the other man's flashlight. "What now?"

"There's a fire in the maintenance barn. Some of the men are moving equipment—"

"That's where the fuel truck is still kept, right?"

"All the big equipment. Jamie said to come get you."

"Let me get my boots on. Damn, I can't go, I have to stay here."

"I'll stay if you want."

"No. Wait, okay, that's a good idea."

Pierce walked back into the room and switched on the lantern. He pulled on his boots as he spoke. "Just stay out in the hallway, outside this door. Are you armed?"

"No—"

"Then take the revolver," Pierce said, handing the gun to the man in the hall.

Pierce grabbed his shotgun and coat off the bed, pulled on his hat, then paused by Analise's bed. "You heard?"

"Yes."

"I'll be back as soon as I can. Don't open that door for anyone but me."

They both turned to the window when they heard a muffled explosion.

"Go," Analise urged, freeing herself of the bedding.

"Come behind me and lock the door."

She padded across the floor and did as he asked. The room was cold. She dressed in warm clothes including wool socks and wrapped a blanket around her shoulders, seating herself on the chair by the window where she could see if a building suddenly shot up in flames.

She must have fallen asleep because suddenly she heard a voice.

Toby.

It was still dark, but he was calling to her. Where was Bierta? Taking the lantern off the bureau, Analise went to the door.

"Toby? Is that you?"

"Analise, I'm scared. Let me in."

Without pause, she responded to the fright in his voice and yanked open the door.

Toby wasn't alone.

Chapter Ten

The rising sun brought a slew of modest miracles as far as Pierce was concerned. For one, the snow had abated. Not stopped, but slowed way down. This was excellent news on a host of fronts. The police and emergency people could arrive and start an investigation into Darrell's murder, the fire marshal could come out and investigate the fire, the helicopter could take all these visitors away—among them a killer—and he could get on with things like calling the insurance company and talking to his father and finding alternate housing for a ton of equipment currently scattered on the snow-covered field.

They'd managed to save most of it by moving it out of the building, but half the building itself was gone. When the fire had spread to a pile of tires and a few propane tanks, they'd lost most of the roof.

Thankfully, no livestock had been close by.

But how had it started in the first place? This

building was a quarter mile from the pavilion where they'd held the campout so a stray spark wasn't responsible. No one worked out here on a stormy night, no equipment had been left running.

Jamie speculated some cowhand got careless with a cigarette butt, but that seemed unlikely to Pierce. He didn't know enough about fires to be able to tell if an accelerant had been used but his guess was that in light of Darrell's murder, they were looking at arson.

He'd told Jamie about the murder and watched as the older man shook his head. "There's never been anyone killed on the Open Sky," he'd said. "Your father is going to blow a gasket."

Of course, there was another possibility and Pierce intended to investigate it. The bodyguard was a smoker, a newcomer, a relative unknown or so it would seem. Had he started the fire, either purposefully as part of a diversion of some kind? Or maybe he'd awoken from where Lucas had stuck him, wandered out to the equipment barn, lit up and kaplooey.

Pierce was anxious to make sure Brad Harley was where he was supposed to be and also to bring his father up to date on events. No doubt the old man had heard all the commotion last night and who knew what Pauline had told him.

Jamie was taking care of ranch business, assigning crew to use the big tractors to haul feed to the herd. Pierce could remember a similar storm that had arrived a few weeks later right at the height of calving season back when he was in high school. No one had slept for the better part of a month, so it could be worse.

Glancing up, however, he had to admit the chances were good the weather would turn again sooner rather than later. As it was, he kept to the plowed roads between buildings, meeting up with Jamie again midpoint and holding a brief conversation.

As he continued on, he looked up at the house to the window of the room where Analise slept, and a smile made its way to his lips. He could live to be eight hundred years old and he would never forget how she'd looked tumbling out of bed in the middle of the night wearing damn near nothing, her nipples hard against her sexy top thanks to the cold room, her black hair floating around her face and shoulders.

Whew.

The woman was an eyeful. It flitted through his mind that he might be able to romance her into a night of passion if there was time and if circumstances didn't continue to conspire to make her visit into a nightmare.

His cell rang as he walked into the barn where Lucas Garvey and the others had stashed the bodyguard. He could see by the caller ID that it was his partner, Bob Turner.

"They've upped the offer," Bob said.

"Not a good time for a chat," Pierce grumbled.

"But Unitex added twenty percent."

"And Sue is pressuring you to get married and start a family. She wants to raise kids in the same town you both grew up in. I know this."

"Maybe what you don't understand is that I want the same things," Bob said softly.

Whoa. No, he hadn't understood that, not really. Maybe he could buy out Bob's share and run the company by himself. He could do it if he gave up things like eating for a couple of years.

"Don't you think about settling down, Pierce?"

"No."

"I can't believe you still enjoy being on the road eleven months out of twelve."

"I settled down once," Pierce said. Hadn't he just had this conversation with the princess the night before?

"Yeah, well, it doesn't have to be something you just do once, buddy."

Pierce had stopped walking as he talked, and stood there in the middle of the barn, head down, studying the toes of his ash-covered boots. Had there always been that note of longing in Bob's voice?

Yes...you've ignored it. You've recognized it and ignored it, you jerk.

"Give me until tomorrow to see if I can buy you out," he said at last. "If I can't swing it, okay, we'll sell and go our separate ways."

"We wouldn't have to," Bob said quickly. "We could be partners again. With what we get for Westin-Turner, we could start over. I mean, the contract stipulates we couldn't go into direct competition with the new owners, but we could stay stateside. Sue has lots of family in Montana. Who knows, she might be able to set you up with someone nice. You'd be closer to home."

Home.

"I'll call you tomorrow night," Pierce promised, then pocketed the cell.

"One disaster at a time," he muttered aloud, looking up and catching the eye of the pinto. He gave Sam a pat and moved on past Jamie's bay mare, then past two more horses to the last three stalls that were usually kept empty to store feed and tack. No bodyguard. No sign there had ever been a bodyguard. The man was an enigma.

Or maybe he was something worse. Maybe he was behind everything that had happened, alone or perhaps in collusion with another one of the princess's party. Just because he'd been hired after the attack on the original bodyguard didn't mean he was in the clear, and being a drunk wasn't much of an excuse, either.

Why sabotage the generator unless it was to decoy Darrell who he'd been seen talking to not long before the murder? But why kill Darrell?

As Pierce turned to get the conversation with his father over with, Sassy Sally walked into the barn. At six foot even and built like the Vegas showgirl she'd once been for a couple of years, she was always an eyeful, but this morning, she was really something. Hours of work dealing with fire and smoke had left her sooty and rumpled, and her platinum hair stuck out in a hundred directions.

"Take the morning off," Pierce said. "You earned it."

"I will after I muck out a few stalls and feed these guys," she said, gesturing at the horses who had all stuck their heads over their gates and were making hungry noises in their throats.

"Did you happen to run into the bodyguard?"

She grabbed a pitchfork. "Mr. Sunglasses? Nope. Haven't seen him since last night. You know who else I haven't seen? Darrell."

It was on the tip of his tongue to tell her about Darrell's murder, but he decided against it. Fact was he was kind of surprised Lucas hadn't told anyone before getting stuck inside the house all night. He'd kept his word. Lucas Garvey seemed to be made of better stuff than his brother, Doyle.

"The bodyguard passed out drunk in the snow after the party," he told her.

"First I heard of it."

As he crossed the yard, Pierce gazed into the gray sky again. Were the clouds thicker, had the temperature dropped again? Where the hell were the police? He took a moment to plow through the deeper snow and make sure the lock on the generator shack was still in place. As he rattled it, his mind zapped back to the gate he'd found with the cut chain. Had that really been only twenty-fours before?

A few minutes later, he was standing in his father's small cabin, sidling up to the fire, his fingers tingling as they defrosted. Melted snow dripped from the brim of his hat so he took it off and hooked it atop the fireplace poker to dry off. "I'm calling the fire department," he said after his brief report. "They can investigate the cause."

"But you didn't call them last night," his father said.

"No. The storm was too big for them to get here. We dealt with it ourselves." He took a deep breath and added, "There's something else you should know about."

It took him only a few moments to relate what had happened to Darrell. His father grew very still as he spoke, his eyes watchful. He'd been eating eggs and bacon, but he laid his fork aside as though news of a murder on Open Sky land stole away his appetite. Pierce didn't blame him one bit.

"I'm not sure what to say," Birch Westin said after Pierce finished. "Hell of a thing to happen. You called the police?"

"They'll be here today."

His old man's gaze darted to the window and the snowy skies outside. "Maybe, maybe not."

"The shed is locked but that's why we're still without power. I don't want to compromise the murder scene."

Birch nodded. "I sure as hell wish Cody or Adam were here."

"So do I. Did you know Darrell?"

"Huh?" Birch looked up from his plate and shook his head. "Know him? Not well. He was new this year. Jamie hired him. Heard someone say he was going with the Lindquist gal. I know of her 'cause she used to hang around the ranch before Darrell got here. Had eyes for one of the other boys, I suppose. Does Pauline know about this?"

"Yes. I asked her not to say anything until I could speak to you myself."

"That might explain why she was so quiet this morning," Birch said.

"I'll try to help her out today," Pierce said.

"That's good. Don't ask that Analise gal to help. Pauline doesn't like other women messing around in her kitchen. Barely tolerated Cody's wife. I had half a mind to make Pauline come live in the cabin with me when your brother got married."

"Why didn't you?" Pierce asked.

"Wouldn't have been proper."

Pierce made sure his lips didn't twitch. "Well, why didn't you marry her then and make it proper?"

He was treated to a swift upward glance from beneath heavy brows. "That's none of your business."

"You're right, it isn't," Pierce said. He picked up his hat. It had warmed up in the few minutes it sat close to the flame and felt good as he pulled it on. "You need anything?"

Birch waved Pierce away with his fork but before Pierce could get out the door, he changed his mind.

"Send Analise over later and we'll play chess again. She beat the socks off me yesterday."

"I'll tell her," Pierce said.

Since when was his father pleased to be beaten at anything?

Chapter Eleven

The house smelled like hot coffee and fresh bread. One thing about ranch life—a man was always hungry and on the Open Sky, at least, the food was plentiful and hearty.

As he sat on the bench in the mudroom and pulled off his muck-encrusted boots and the coat he'd worn which was now covered with soot and smelled like smoke, Pauline opened the connecting door. "I put fresh clothes in the shower room for you."

He glanced at the small bathroom adjoining the mudroom and saw jeans and a shirt folded over the towel rack.

"No offense, but you smell like an ashtray," she added, and closed the door.

No offense taken. He took a brief but scalding shower and put on the clean clothes and felt better for it. In his current line of work, he didn't go around dirty all the time. He wasn't used to this kind of schedule and the truth was he was weary. What he needed was a hearty breakfast and eight hours of uninterrupted sleep.

Pauline met him with a steaming mug of coffee. "That's better," she said approvingly, glancing down at the cleaner version of the same clothes he'd worn the day before right down to the boots which were actually a pair of Adam's. Bonnie, curled up on a rug when he came into the room, shuffled over to wag her tail against his leg. "Who's up and about?"

"The general and the other man. The general came down and ordered rolls and coffee for both of them to be served in his room."

Like she was their damn servant. "And the princess?"

"Still asleep, I guess. The little boy must be plain tuckered out if he's still down, too."

"Lucas have any trouble last night?" Pierce asked as he hooked a warm yeasty roll off the cutting board.

"I guess he had the same trouble as the rest of you with the fire and everything," she said, loading a tray with butter, honey and cutlery, a covered basket of rolls balanced atop the plates.

He gestured at the tray. "This go upstairs? I'll deliver it for you. Lucas wasn't at the fire with us. I left him up in the hall keeping an eye on things."

"The general didn't mention him," Pauline

said. "Wait a second and I'll stick on another mug and some more rolls. The poor boy must be ready to gnaw on his own arm."

"Did the police call?" Pierce asked, lowering his voice.

Pauline's hand trembled as she pulled another red mug from the iron rack. In all the years he'd known her, he'd never seen her cry, and it was a little unnerving to find her eyes filled with tears now. "No, they didn't call, but Miley Lindquist did, wanting to talk to Darrell because he didn't answer his cell phone. I didn't tell her he was... dead. I didn't know if I should. I didn't even mention it to your father and I never keep secrets from him. Those two men up there—one of them murdered Darrell, didn't they? Or maybe it was that awful bodyguard. How can someone as sweet as the princess be surrounded by such people?"

He put an arm around her shoulders. "I don't know who killed Darrell, but to be on the safe side I'm going to ask everyone to stay upstairs until the police can talk to them. That will make more work for you, I'm afraid. Hopefully the cops will get here while there's a break in the weather."

She looked over his shoulder and nodded toward the window. "There goes your break."

His gaze followed hers. It had started to snow again.

He picked up the heavily laden tray and backed out the door, commanding Bonnie to stay with Pauline. Cody's dog was notoriously friendly; still, she might provide some protection for the housekeeper as she went about her chores.

The chair outside the princess's door was empty. Pierce knocked on the general's door with his elbow. Where was Lucas?

The general opened it, dressed already or maybe he never took off the uniform. "You can put that over there," he said, gesturing inside at the desktop. By the way his nose wrinkled, it was obvious to Pierce that he must still smell like ashes and smoke.

"I have things to do, you put it over there," he said, handing off the tray. The general took it, eyebrows arched.

"Have you seen the man who was up here last night? His chair is out here but he's gone," Pierce added.

"I haven't seen anyone."

Pierce swallowed his irritation. Lucas must have needed a break, but he shouldn't have left his post without getting someone to relieve him. "I'm waking everyone up," he said. "We all need to talk before the police arrive."

"Police? Why are the police coming? And why is there still no power?"

"We'll talk in a minute," Pierce said, rapping on Vaughn's door, then moving down the hall. He knocked once on the maid's door to rouse her and the boy, then softly on the princess's door.

If it hadn't been locked from the inside, he might not have knocked. Maybe she was still in bed, and once again the thought of how the silk all but disappeared on her body made him ache. What would it be like to kiss her awake?

He tried the knob and was alarmed when it turned easily in his hand.

The lantern on the desk emitted a very weak yellow light as though it been burning for hours and the batteries were almost dead. The room was empty. In half a dozen steps he was pushing open the bathroom door, knowing she wasn't in there even before his eyes confirmed it.

Turning back into the room, he took in her nightclothes folded on top of the dresser. Nothing looked out of place or askew. Maybe she was in with Toby and the maid but fully dressed? If so, why hadn't she answered their door when he knocked on it?

By now the general and Vaughn were both in the hall, the general holding a mug of coffee. Pierce rapped harder on the maid's door and when there was no response, tried the knob. This door was unlocked, too, and he pushed it open.

The maid was on the floor, hands tied behind her back, legs tied at the ankles. She'd been blindfolded and someone had slapped a piece of duct tape over her mouth. She was wearing what appeared to be moss-green flannel pajamas and she was so still he thought she was dead.

"Bierta!" gasped the general who had come into the room behind Pierce. By that time, Pierce was on his knees, taking the blindfold off the woman on the floor. Her skin was cold to the touch, but the eyes that greeted him were wide open and terrified. Without her eyeglasses she looked younger, softer.

There was no painless way to get tape off someone's mouth. She cried out as the last of it lifted. Pierce took his pocketknife and hacked away at the restraints around her wrists. Her hand flew up to rub her lips as he sawed through the ropes on her ankles.

"Where's the princess? Where's the boy?" he demanded as he helped the woman stand. She sagged when she got to her feet and stumbled toward a chair.

"They took her," she gasped. "They must have taken them both."

"Who's they?"

She shook her head as she pushed brown bangs

away from her brows. "I don't know who they were. I woke up with one of them holding a gun against my neck. He said he had a message for King Thomas. He said they'd warned Princess Analise to tell her father to veto the pipeline bill and they knew she hadn't. They said now it was up to the general to tell the king. They said Princess Analise will be safe if the king vetoes the pipeline. They said when they hear he has done this, they'll release her."

"Were they from Chatioux or were they Americans?"

"I don't know. How could I—"

"Their voices," Pierce explained. "Did they have accents?"

"I don't know," she said again, turning an anguished, myopic gaze up to Pierce. "I was too frightened and then I was trying to remember what they said so I could tell General Kaare. Oh, General, you have to call King Thomas. You have to get him to veto that bill!"

"When is the vote?" Pierce asked.

"Four days from now. We were to have returned home the day after tomorrow in time for the parliament meeting," the general said, pacing now. "I pleaded with the princess to skip this unnecessary side trip to this godforsaken outpost, but she wouldn't listen."

"I am against the pipeline," Vaughn announced. He was still hovering near the door. "I told the princess that. I'll tell the king the same thing. If she'd listened to me, this wouldn't have happened."

Pierce turned to look at the man. "You're the one who drove her and her bodyguard into a trap, aren't you, Mr. Vaughn?"

"That was an accident."

"What we haven't discussed is the fact that the regular driver didn't show up because someone stuck him in the trunk of his car and drove it into Puget Sound. He was found dead yesterday."

The room grew incredibly silent.

"Something else we haven't talked about is the dead man out in our generator shack who was apparently killed as he tried to get the power back on after it was sabotaged," Pierce added with a meaningful look all around.

The silence deepened.

He turned back to Bierta in time to see her folded hands tremble.

"How many of them were there?"

She hesitated before she spoke. "Two, I think. Only one spoke. Maybe he was American. Maybe he wasn't. I don't know, I was so frightened and his voice was a low hiss. They blindfolded me right away and bound me and left me here in the dark."

"How did you get on the floor?" the general barked.

"I tried to stand and fell." She shivered as her teeth rattled together. "The princess has been stolen away in the night. Hours ago, now. You have to call—"

"The princess was your responsibility last night," General Kaare interrupted as he stared into Pierce's eyes.

"You think I don't know that?" Pierce ripped a blanket off the bed and handed it to the maid. "Bierta, right? Bierta, do you have any idea where they took them?"

"None," she said miserably as she pulled the blanket around her shoulders.

"I heard engines," Vaughn volunteered. "Very early this morning. The sound moved away from the house, out that way, toward those mountains."

"Yes, yes, I heard them, too," Bierta said.

Pierce turned to Vaughn. "Did you go to the window and look outside?"

"No. I assumed it was connected to all the other noises last night. First the ruckus in the hall, and then that man out here knocking on your door and your voices. There was an explosion but it was a far way off—"

"That was from the fire. That's why you heard voices. One of my men came to get me, I left him on guard here and now he's missing, too. How long after the voices did you hear the engines?"

"An hour maybe."

That's a hell of a head start, Pierce thought with alarm.

Looking down his nose, Kaare cleared his throat. "If any harm befalls Princess Analise, the king will hold you personally responsible."

"Let's worry about the king later," Pierce muttered as his gaze strayed to the window and the storm outside. Through the snow he could just make out parallel tracks leading away from the house, away from the ranch, toward the mountains and the lake beyond. Feeling the first stirring of hope, he moved closer to the window and peered down.

Snowmobiles?

He turned back to see the other two men deep in hushed conversation by the door. They looked up as though they felt his gaze on them. "I'm having trouble believing neither one of you heard two men hauling away two or three hostages," Pierce growled.

"This is a noisy, poorly run ranch," the general said. "When you arbitrarily issued orders last night, I put in earplugs."

Pierce ran a hand through his hair and rubbed the back of his neck. "Okay. For now, I want you all to stay in your rooms until the cops get here."

"That's impossible," Kaare protested. "I need to phone Chatioux. The king must be told at once."

"Fine, phone him, then come back here until the cops arrive."

"Where are you going?" Kaare demanded.

"I'm going to go find the princess," he said, kind of surprised anyone had to ask.

"No," Vaughn and Kaare said in unison.

The general added, "We must consult the king first."

"Yes," Vaughn said, chiming in. "They told Bierta the princess would be released after her father vetoes the bill. Any show of force by one of us could be misconstrued."

"They'll kill her, I know they will," Bierta cried.

Pierce looked at each of them in turn. "You don't bargain with terrorists. You don't trust them, either."

The general returned Pierce's gaze with fierce focus. "I forbid you to go."

Pierce shook his head and turned to leave.

"The princess will die in this storm," Bierta mumbled through her tears.

"Not if I can help it," Pierce said under his breath. The woman's cries grew hysterical as he left the room. Vaughn stood aside to let him pass, his narrow face pinched.

Pierce met Pauline on the stairs.

"What's going on up there?"

"All hell is breaking loose. The police here?"

"No. I came running because of all the racket."

"I hate to do this to you, but I need your help with these people." He briefly explained what was going on, finishing with, "I don't know where Lucas is but knowing what happened to Darrell, I'm not holding out much hope."

"Oh, my goodness. That poor girl. First Darrell and now Lucas."

"What girl? Who are you talking about?"

"Miley Lindquist."

Pierce tried to clear his head. He had to get moving. "Did you hear an engine noise late in the night?"

"No. But I sleep like the dead, you know that. I didn't even know about the fire until Jamie told me this morning."

"I need you to go up there and keep everyone from killing each other. I'll send someone to help you. I'm taking Jamie with me."

"Taking him where? Where are you going?"

"To find the princess and the kid and hopefully Lucas Garvey. If the police manage to get here, try to explain what's going on. You better call them now and report this situation, too. Go get a weapon out of the case. The combination for the lock is in Cody's desk."

"I'll get Sassy Sally to help me. She can calm a rattlesnake. You just save the princess and that sweet little boy." By the grim set of Pauline's mouth, it was clear she meant business.

So did he.

He glanced back up the stairs as he turned in time to see the retreating back of a man hurry down the hall. Had he been eavesdropping? Did it matter?

Vaughn of Kaare? He couldn't tell in the dismal light.

Chapter Twelve

By the time Pierce collected a couple of guns from the cabinet, he found Jamie coming across the yard under a full head of steam, fists clenched at his sides, mouth set in a grimace.

"I was just comin' to get you," Jamie yelled in greeting. He hadn't changed clothes but he had found time to wash away the worst of the fire residue. "Someone got into the barn and disabled every snowmobile and four-wheeler they didn't outright steal. Who in tarnation would do something like that?"

There went plan A: *follow—fast.* "I should have anticipated this."

Jamie's forehead wrinkled. "What are you talking about?"

Once again, Pierce explained. The need to get going churned acid in his stomach.

"They took the little boy, too?" Jamie sighed. "They took Tex?"

"It looks like it. That leaves us on horseback.

I'll saddle up while you detail a couple of men to search the ranch in case the tracks are decoys and the hostages are still around here. Lucas Garvey is missing, too. They should keep watch for him, dead or alive. My phone coverage in Wyoming stinks. You tell them to call you if they find anything. Oh, and get someone else to get the equipment moved in case the weather deteriorates again and remind everyone this is a cattle ranch which means take care of the herd. Get some additional cake out to the cows. They'll need all the food they can get."

"Will do."

"Can you tell how many vehicles are missing?"

"At least two. One of the trailers is gone. Mike found the mess when he went to take a scooter out to the feeding shelter. I told him to use one of the tractors instead. Good thing they didn't all burn up last night."

Pierce knew it all had to be connected. "Meet me in ten minutes. We have to get out of here before the new snow completely covers the tracks."

By the time Jamie returned, Pierce had gathered emergency supplies and saddled three horses, taking a spare gelding just in case they needed him. He'd made a return journey to the weapon cabinet and both horses were outfitted with rifle scabbards. Pierce was also wearing a leg holster and carried the Smith and Wesson .38.

He and Jamie swung into their saddles and rode out into the snow, Pierce out in front, Jamie astride his mare, trailing the extra horse. They paused when Pauline flagged them down.

"Those people are impossible," she said through chattering teeth. "They're all over the house doing any darn thing they want. I've half a mind to go get Birch and wheel him into the house. He could make them listen. Here, I packed you some food. You boys be careful."

Pierce thanked Pauline as he stuffed the food in his saddlebag, then took off. They rounded the frozen pond where they picked up the fading trail made hours earlier and which was quickly vanishing in the snow.

However, there were just so many places someone could escape to in this kind of weather. The Open Sky was miles from anywhere. There was a chance, he supposed, that some sort of transport had managed to get close enough during the storm to whisk everyone away, but he thought that unlikely. He was pretty sure Harley would be at the center of this, maybe with an accomplice who was local and that meant the kidnapping was probably opportunistic and the retreat had been toward the lake. Open Sky land ended thirty or forty miles further on—was that where they were headed? The town of Woodwind was over there...

If there was a transport of some kind involved, all bets were off, they could be anywhere by now. But if they'd been forced to keep it local, it narrowed down the opportunities for shelter.

The first structure they'd come across would be Adam's half-finished house on the western shore of the now-frozen lake. The second would be the ice fishing shanty. The third was a barn on the southern shore. That's where Pierce thought it likely they'd headed. That would keep them close to the lake for air transport once the weather cleared, plus it would provide shelter.

Wait, there was another destination but it would take local knowledge; the old Indian burial cave was about five miles from the eastern shore. The tribe was long extinct, its name even lost, the site now safeguarded and tended by the Westin family as it had been for the past hundred and twenty years. Adam led regular attempts to get their father to invite the university to excavate and protect the site but Birch Westin would have none of it. "It's ours to take care of," their father always blustered when challenged. "We don't need no damn outsiders telling us what to do on Open Sky land."

Thanks to the compacted snow under the snowmobile imprints, the horses were able to move along at a pretty good clip. Still, the conditions were dangerous for the animals so they kept their pace slow. The snow gathered on hat brims as the men looked down at their gloved hands gripping reins and saddle horns, trying to protect their faces from the wind-driven elements.

Warm, sunny Italy seemed like a lifetime and a world away.

It took the better part of an hour to get to Adams's building site. The house itself was two stories high though only partially visible as it stood in amidst a stand of leafless quaking aspen on a small promontory. The snowmobile tracks had long since faded so they had no way of knowing if they were riding into danger or not, but there was such an abandoned look to the place it was impossible to think anyone was inside the empty shell.

"They'd be burning something in the fireplace trying to stay warm," Jamie said, looking up at the chimney. "No smoke."

Still, they approached it from the shadows of the evergreen trees and were alternately comforted and disappointed when they got to the overhang on the porch and found no traces of snowy footprints or snowmobile tracks.

"We'll have to search both it and the outbuildings," Pierce said, "to make sure no one got left behind here."

"I'll take the barn," Jamie said, sliding off the mare and tying her and the gelding in a protected spot next to Pierce's pinto. Melting snow made streaks down his sooty cheeks. He produced a huge red bandana to wipe at himself as he walked off toward the barn.

Drawing his gun, Pierce opened the door to his brother Adam's new house.

The inside walls had all been framed, the windows installed, the plumbing and electricity in place. Adam had chosen traditional construction as opposed to a log house. Pierce drew out the pocket flashlight he carried and used it to quickly walk through the heavily shadowed rooms, then climbed the stairs to the second floor and searched up there. He found no sign anyone had been here since the building season ended the fall before. A brief glance out one of the windows gave him a good view of the frozen lake. He saw nothing traveling on it.

Though the house was little more than a skeleton now, Pierce knew by next year at this time, it would be pretty great. Adam was the consummate craftsman and he would make every inch of this place special. Some local cowgirl was going to get the house of her dreams one of these days—if Adam ever bumped into her.

Jamie was standing in what would someday be the main living area, stamping the snow from his boots in front of a huge rock fireplace that had never seen a fire.

"Nothing?" he asked, glancing up at Pierce.

Pierce re-holstered the gun. "Nothing. Same with the barn?"

"Just the stuff that's supposed to be there but I could only tell that through the windows. Place is locked up tighter than a drum."

"Then it's time we get going," Pierce said, alarmed at how long everything was taking. The two men once again mounted their horses and continued on in the driving snow.

The tracks were gone by now but way out on the frozen lake, Pierce could make out the bright yellow of the ice fishing shanty and that brought a clear memory of Princess Analise wondering if the ice shanty was charming. Her blue eyes had sparkled like a damn bubbling brook as she'd asked him even though she'd been worried and scared someone wanted to kill her.

Who could want to harm her, especially for some pipeline? It was crazy.

He closed his eyes for a second as the horse walked slowly across the snow-covered ice. Until that moment, he'd been so caught up in starting a search that he hadn't allowed himself to think about what she and boy were going through.

They must be terrified.

Another hour passed. He was frozen clear through, his face so numb it had lost all feeling, the frigid air traveling up his sleeves, ice crystals clinging to the brim of his hat. Years before, his grandfather had used horse-drawn carts to cut blocks of ice from the frozen lake to store for the summer. Right now, his feet felt like two of those blocks.

The yellow building grew larger. Pierce turned in the saddle to reassure himself Jamie was still behind him. Both the old man and the horses plodded ahead with heads down as though on remote. The wind blew snow around the horses' feet, their long tails and manes flying.

When they were close enough to be a target, Pierce pulled Sam to a stop. He got out of the saddle and walked back to Jamie.

"I can't figure any way to look inside that thing that doesn't require one of us to sidle on up and open the door. There's nothing to hide behind out here. You cover me with the rifle. I'm going in."

Jamie got off his horse. He was a crack shot but his hands had to be as frozen as Pierce's were and Pierce was beginning to wonder if he could even hold a gun, let alone pull the trigger.

As Jamie got ready, Pierce did his best not to drop the handgun he wrested once again from the holster and started the nerve-racking walk toward the shanty.

Besides the rattling of the old door as the wind assaulted it, nothing made a sound. The shanty had one window but it was opaque with age and soot. He stayed low once he reached the yellow siding and looking back, could barely make out Jamie and the three horses through the blowing snow.

Under the small overhang near the door, he discovered the imprint of shoes and his heartbeat scooted into hyperdrive. Someone was here, or had been here.

Further study revealed the tracks doubled back until they disappeared in the new snow. Maybe this had been the original destination but it was too small and cold for what they had in mind.

What did they have in mind? And who was *they?* If *they* wanted to use the princess to force her father into doing what they wanted, why take Lucas and Toby, too?

Stop stalling, he told himself, and flexing his fingers inside the leather gloves, gripped the gun, grabbed the doorknob and turned it. In one swift movement, he banged against the door so hard it hit the wall behind it.

It took him a second to make sense of what he saw.

Chaos. Utter chaos, as though a war had been

fought within the square footage of a small bedroom. Shattered shelves, fishing gear, canned
food and rustic furniture spread from one end
to the other. And at the center of this mayhem,
the hole in the ice, usually capped with a wooden
disk, today plugged with a human being.

Pierce made his way through the rubble, his
stomach stampeding up his throat. It wasn't the
stench of certain death that repelled him—it was
too cold for foul odors to flourish here. What
disturbed him was the sight of a man stuffed
headfirst into the frigid water below the ice, his
arms flailed out to the sides, visible burns on one
wrist where the sleeve had ridden up, a flash of
white thigh and frozen blood showing through
a slash in his jeans.

It was the obscenity of it.

Pierce immediately holstered the gun and
knelt to pull on the man's massive shoulders.
He knew it was the princess's bodyguard even
before he finally freed Harley's head because of
the man's size and black clothes. It was obvious
from the condition of the back of his skull that
he'd been hit from behind. Though the wound
was bloodless now thanks to the frigid water,
hair and tissue coated the upended bottom of a
nearby cast-iron skillet abandoned in the debris.

Pierce half expected to find Harley's dark
glasses still in place despite the conditions. But

as he turned the bodyguard over, he found the sunglasses gone, the sightless eyes open and slightly startled-looking. Just as Bierta had appeared without her distorting thick lenses, Harley looked oddly vulnerable.

Sensing movement nearby, Pierce stood abruptly, spinning around, drawing out his gun as he moved. Frozen fingers or not, he was ready to pull the trigger.

Chapter Thirteen

Analise groaned.

Where was she? Why did her head throb?

Why did her stomach ache, why did her bones hurt, why couldn't she feel her hands and feet? Why was she in the dark, bouncing, thumping against metal, something heavy and cold weighing her down like a shroud?

And what was that noise?

An engine. Maybe two. They were out of synch with each other.

She was with those men.

It came back in dizzying pieces.

Toby calling her name. Her flinging open the door. Him standing on her threshold, face ashen in the reflection of the lantern on her desk, tears rolling down his cheeks. A sudden bright light from behind and above him had blinded her and she'd seen the flash of a gun. Toby whisked away, a man wearing a mask, coming like a black shadow.

Oblivion.

"Toby?" she whispered.

She couldn't even hear her voice. She said his name again, louder.

Nothing. Where was he?

She tried changing positions from her side to her back. Something was poking into her hip and it hurt. But it was too cramped to move; she was stuck. The heavy blanket thing on top of her...

That's when she realized her wrists and ankles were bound and that she was blindfolded, too. And then she remembered the shack.

The shack. She'd awoken first in a small enclosure with Toby dumped next to her, both of them dazed. There'd been shouting and noise all around them and she'd covered his body with hers, pushing him into a far corner, trying to protect him. It had been like being in the middle of a stampede of crazed bulls on the narrow streets of Pamplona.

She'd been blindfolded and gagged but Toby had use of his hands and he'd hugged her fiercely. She could still recall the pressure of his small arms around her neck. Wait, he'd been tied at the wrists, too. When they'd pulled him away from her, the rope tying his hands together had caught and pulled at her hair.

It was all so fuzzy.

The thing on top of her weighed a ton. It

smelled slightly of mold. A tarp, she decided. Canvas maybe, and damp.

What had they given her to make her so logy?

Toby must be in a similar situation very close by. She had to get to him again and reassure him. He'd been so frightened.

What was that thing biting into her hip? She groped with frozen hands until she felt something even colder than her fingers.

For one second she didn't even dare to breathe. There was no doubt about it—what she felt was a gun. A tiny one, smaller than her hand, but a gun.

How could this be? Someone must have dropped it. She didn't know enough about guns to fumble with it in the dark. Was it loaded? If she tried to check, she might end up shooting herself. But what a miracle. A gun!

Where in the world could she hide it? The possibilities were few and far between. She couldn't get it up a sleeve—the rope they'd bound her with made that impossible. Maybe she could reach one of her rear pockets... It would create a bulge, but maybe her coat would cover it. How about her boot? They were pretty snug, but maybe...

In the end, the pocket won simply because nothing else worked. But stuffed in there, it created a worse discomfort than ever and she tried hard to roll onto her side.

For a second, she drifted away again. She was in Chatioux. Spring would arrive in a few weeks. Wild pansies would dot the meadow above the castle. As the days grew warmer, the waterfalls would begin to tumble down steep cliffs, dozens and dozens of them, roaring with the freshest, purest water in the world that would pool in rock basins. How she yearned to dip cupped hands into that water and drink deeply.

It would be too cold to swim, and yet the thought of sliding through water was intoxicating. She could go to the lake near the castle. The water would be warm and welcoming...

She thought of Pierce touching her chin, her cheeks, his hands strong but gentle.

What if she died today? Wasn't it a shame she hadn't spent the night before in his arms? Wasn't it a waste? Technically, she was a damn virgin. Saved for a man who didn't love her with whom to have perfect children who might now never be born.

And she would gladly trade all of it for one hour in Pierce Westin's bed.

Too late.

Unless he came after her.

Her heart thumped wildly at the thought but she abandoned it at once. She knew how these things worked. The kidnappers would promise she would be returned safely if her father did whatever it was they wanted, namely vote down the pipeline.

General Kaare would call her father. Her father would be made to chose between his daughter and the welfare of his people. He would make the decision that was right. She was a big girl, she knew the stakes, she expected no less of him. Too much hung in the balance...

But what about Toby? Would he become a bargaining chip to use against Analise? Would his life be sacrificed like Darrell's life had been?

No.

They were coming to some kind of destination. She could tell because the engine noise had ratcheted down and the speed was decreasing. Her stomach turned over as the world suddenly became very silent.

Be brave for Toby's sake....

"Get her out of there," a man said, and a second later a blast of cold fresh air announced the lifting of the tarp. Someone grabbed her jacket and pulled her upward, hauling her to her feet. Cold wind blew snow against her face and whipped her hair around her head, but she was still blindfolded and could see nothing. Still, it felt wonderful. Before she could steady herself, someone tipped her over his shoulder and turned abruptly, banging her head against something hard and she cried out.

"Haven't you done enough damage for one day?" the other man snapped.

"Screw you!" the man carrying her grumbled. He had a deep voice with undercurrents of excitement. She couldn't identify either voice. Not Harley, that's all she knew for certain.

With her butt on top of the man's shoulder, would he notice the gun? Hopefully the arduous steps he took as he plowed through the deep snow would keep him occupied. She could tell he wasn't a beefy man like Harley or as muscular as Pierce, but he was strong and his grip on her legs was like a vise. Behind her, she could hear the crunch of another man walking. Was he carrying Toby?

They climbed stairs, then a door opened. The room they entered was out of blowing wind and snow, but it was almost as cold. Her captor's footsteps thudded across what sounded like a wooden floor. He rolled her off his shoulder and she dropped a couple of feet onto what felt and smelled like moldy straw. Before she hit the ground, however, she heard the clatter of metal.

Instantly knowing what had happened, she tried to twist her body to grasp with her bound hands in the direction of the noise.

"Looking for this, darlin'?" the deep voice demanded and she could imagine him holding the gun she'd found earlier. His breath smelled like liquor.

"Where did that come from?" the other man demanded.

"Our little princess is full of surprises," the drinker said as his footsteps moved away from her. There was a metallic click, and then a laugh. "It's loaded, too. Watch out."

Damn. She'd just lost a loaded gun.

Both men lowered their voices and she couldn't make out what they said.

She tried articulating Toby's name around the gag. The drinker was suddenly closer. "What's that? You worried about something?"

She said Toby's name again.

"Is that the little fella? Let me tell you about him, darlin'." But before he could utter another word, he was suddenly pulled away and the sounds of yet another scuffle erupted around her. It ended with a thump in a far corner.

"Keep your big mouth shut, you understand me?" the man who must have been carrying Toby said. "Things are already screwed up because of you." He sounded out of breath and furious.

"It wasn't my fault—"

"*Nothing* is ever your fault."

"I'm about froze to death. I'm going to start a fire."

"Fire makes smoke."

"So what? No one's coming after her."

"Don't count on that. We never counted on Pierce Westin being here and he's got a thing for this girl. It's as plain as the nose on his face. He'll come if he can."

"Just like you would for Miley?"

"Don't use any names, you idiot."

"You know, poor little Miley is going to mighty lonely now. She'll need comforting, and for once in your sorry life, you'll have a little money to spend on her."

"I said shut up!"

Another scuffle erupted.

Except for heavy breathing, it grew quiet again. Finally, Analise heard the clatter of wood as though logs had been tumbled to the floor.

"I'm still cold," the drinker grumbled.

"Do what you want. I'm going up to the loft and get myself a good spot to shoot at anyone who comes around," the other said. "Just keep your hands off the princess. The deal is she goes back in one piece."

Once again Analise said Toby's name as loud and clearly as she could manage. Footsteps approached. "You want the boy safe?" the man who had just announced he was leaving said softly. "Then sit tight and cooperate. You want to go back to your palace and see your daddy again, then be careful."

"And hope your daddy loves you," the drinker added.

The door opened, sending a waft of freezing air into the room, then it slammed.

"It's just you and me, darlin'," the gruff one said, but his voice sounded as though he was still at a distance.

Analise squared her shoulders. She pushed away fear. So far she hadn't been allowed to see anyone, surely that meant they intended to honor their promise to return her unharmed. Hopefully Toby was also blindfolded. Blindfolds were their tickets home.

Where was Toby?

Was he even in this room?

She held her breath and listened for a sound that would announce his presence or a sense of movement apart from the thuds and sputters the man made while starting the fire.

What about the journey between the snowmobile and the house? She'd been a little dazed from the knock on her head but she remembered footsteps behind her. The opening door, the fall to the hay, the clatter of the lost gun…

No sound of Toby, she was almost sure of it.

Where was Toby?

PIERCE DIDN'T TURN when he heard footsteps at the door of the shanty. In a soft voice, he called, "That you, Jamie?"

"Yeah. I wondered what was taking you so long. What in the hell happened here? Is that the bodyguard?"

"Yeah. Someone hit him over the head and drowned him for good measure. Right now my concern is what's going on over here."

Jamie was at his side in a few steps. As they both approached a corner littered with blankets, they heard a soft moan.

"Someone is under that blanket," Pierce said. "I'll cover you."

Jamie instantly tore away the blanket. Princess Analise's cousin lay curled on his side, his breathing shallow and labored, his freckles stark again his paleness. His wrists were bound before him.

"What did they do to the poor little guy?" Jamie muttered, his voice choked with emotion. There was a bump on the child's head, dried blood matted his red hair. Jamie worked at the knot on the boy's wrists.

All this took just seconds, but in those seconds, Pierce traveled back nine years to the crib of his son, Patrick. He remembered every detail of that moment. Indeed, he'd spent years trying to forget but there were some things you didn't forget, not ever.

"We have to get him back to the ranch," Pierce muttered, his own voice raspy. Why had the kidnappers left the child here in this shape? Where was Princess Analise? "He needs medical care. Is Doc Hampstead still living at Three Corners?"

"Doc died a couple of years ago. Sally is a certified EMT. Maybe she can figure something out."

"Call the ranch," Pierce said, and spent the minutes Jamie used on his phone to gently wrap the boy in thick wool blankets until about all that showed was his pallid face.

So innocent...

"Pauline says they finished searching the ranch and didn't find Lucas or anyone else. The police phoned. They're on their way. She says Doc Hampstead's daughter is doing a residency in Missoula but she thinks she's home on some kind of break. She'll take care of getting the gal to the ranch. Apparently Mike got some of the vehicles working."

"That's great," Pierce said. "You take the gelding, he'll be fresher. I'll take Sam and the mare."

"Take them where?"

"I have to keep looking, Jamie. You know that."

"But—"

"You can get the boy back to the ranch as fast without me as you can with me."

"But I have a compass. I can find my way in this blizzard, and you..."

"Don't waste time arguing with me."

Jamie nodded. "You're as stubborn as Birch. Okay. After I get the boy to safety I'll come back—"

"No," Pierce said. They'd been moving outside to the horses as they spoke. Jamie climbed up on the gelding and Pierce handed up the still child, tucking blankets around his head as Jamie cradled him in his arms. "Bad enough one of us is wandering around out in this. Stay put. Don't leave the boy alone with anyone from Chatioux."

"Pauline says they've scattered like stray calves. She doesn't know where the hell they all are."

"Be careful," Pierce said, and patting the gelding's rump, watched as Jamie disappeared into the snow.

As Pierce closed the shanty door, his gaze once again landed on the dead bodyguard. This time he caught sight of something gold glittering in the man's hand and went inside to check it out. He found a fine gold chain twisted in Harley's fingers, a small diamond flower cupped in his hand.

The princess's necklace.

He pried it from the dead man's grasp, dreading what—or who—he would find next. Lucas Garvey bleeding to death in the snow? Analise? But why hurt her?

Then again, why kill Darrell, why kill Harley?

And who was in on it with Harley?

Anger chasing away weariness, he left behind the shanty and the secrets it held.

Chapter Fourteen

Somehow Analise managed to fall asleep. She awoke with a start as something slipped from her face.

A man squatted in front of her. As she gasped through the gag, he ran a finger down her cheek. "What's the matter, darlin'? Startle you?"

Her blindfold dangled from his other hand.

She shook her head, frantically searching the room for Toby. There wasn't a single indication he'd ever been there.

"How about you give me a little of what you're giving Pierce Westin," the man said.

She shook her head again. Her neck and shoulders ached from the tension of having her arms pulled so tight behind her, wrists laced together.

He produced a large pocketknife and popped out the blade. "I can use this to convince you to be friendly or I can use it to cut that gag and give you something to eat and drink. Your choice, darlin'."

Analise squeezed her eyes shut, but the man's lascivious grin was just as vivid with her eyes closed as it was with them open. He had dark hair cut poorly, falling over a thin, weathered face. Small eyes and mouth, bigger than average nose, red blotches of high color on his cheeks emphasizing old scars of juvenile acne. His breath smelled more than ever of spirits. He must have been drinking as she nodded off.

Her eyes opened as his fingers slid down her throat. He caught the tab of her coat zipper and pulled it down, and then his hands reached under her jacket, under her shirt, grasping at her breasts. Spit glistened on his thin lips.

There was nothing she could do to stop him short of squirming away and this she did. To her dismay, her measly fighting efforts seemed to arouse him and the next thing she knew, he'd clenched her throat in one hand while throwing her flat on her back, arms pinned beneath her.

"That's how you want it, darlin'? Rough? That's fine with me."

A blast of cold air announced the door opening and for one wild incredible moment, Analise expected Pierce to materialize. She twisted her neck and caught a glimpse of a man who looked much like the one groping her. The newcomer raced across the floor with a rifle held at his side. He tore Analise's attacker away.

"Damn it, Doyle. Do you always have to mess everything up?"

Analise recognized the man who had just rescued her. He'd been the one who came to her room last night, the one who told Pierce about the fire...

Lucas.

He was staring down at her and by the expression in his eyes, she could tell he knew she'd identified him.

"Damn it," he repeated, kicking Doyle who had fallen into a sitting position a few feet away. Raising his head like an angry wolf in the wild, he repeated, "Damn it! You had to see the fear in her eyes, didn't you? You had to ruin everything."

"Just a dang minute," Doyle said, laboriously getting to his feet. "I'm the one who got us this gig. I'm the one they approached, I'm the one who made the deal, I'm the one who's going to make you rich, little brother."

"That's cause you're the one who spends all his time down at Clancy's. Some of us have actual jobs."

"You call freezing your ass off searching for stray cows a good time, be my guest, go back to it."

"I can't go back," Lucas said. "You know that. Especially now that the princess recognizes me."

Doyle laughed as he stared down at Analise, then back at Lucas. "Do you really think she's going to live to tell the tale? Use your head, dude. She's a dead woman."

Lucas didn't look convinced, but the glance he cast Analise was murderous. He turned to Doyle and said, "Just put your coat on and come outside. I need help hiding the snowmobiles."

"What about her?"

"She's trussed up like a calf at a rodeo. She won't go nowhere."

THE WORLD WAS a cold, miserable place, more white than anything Pierce had ever seen, even when he was a kid. What he wouldn't give to have either or both of his brothers with him. Where in the heck was Cody?

Through the falling snow he finally saw the wooden sides of the eastern feed barn. The ranch produced a lot of its own hay during the short summer; to not do so would mean buying feed and that meant tens of thousands of dollars. The best quality was tucked away in weatherproof structures like this one and distributed throughout the winter. Growing hay was as integral a part of ranching as growing cows.

He approached on the sly and entered using the stalls in the far back. He brought the horses in out of the snow, too, letting them eat from the bountiful store of feed. Leaving them there, he took the rifle from its scabbard and made his way between rolled towers of hay, the smells bringing summer harvest back to mind.

Was that the first positive memory he'd had about this place since getting here? No, there were others. Riding Sam out to check the fences, the smell of the kitchen on a cold morning, the huge sky that could be ominous like it was now or as crisp and blue as the Mediterranean. The jagged mountains, the trees, the pure clean air and the satisfaction of working hard.

He moved slowly and quietly, listening as he inched his way along. Was that a creak in the loft? Hard to tell. The wind made a lot of things groan and squeak.

By the time he neared the open area in front he knew he was alone. Stepping into the narrow clearing proved his senses hadn't misled him. No one had been here for quite a while, the doors were closed, the air was cold but undisturbed.

No princess.

He sat down on a wooden bench and put his head in his hands, closing his eyes. Fatigue and weariness were catching up with him and he didn't know what to do next. His stomach had gone beyond hunger to no-man's-land but the thought of eating what Pauline had sent made him cringe. The Indian site seemed a remote and improbable possibility, but that's all he could think of. He'd go there next.

He threw his head back against the wall, smothering a yawn in his fist. His mind conjured up the image of the ranch office the afternoon before. The princess seated in the big chair, him perched on the desk. She'd looked so pretty sitting there, even as scared as she'd been. Maybe when you were born royal you figured out how to command any room; her delicate aura had dwarfed the heavy, masculine office furniture.

He stared straight ahead. *The furniture.* What was his tired brain trying to tell him? He rubbed his eyes and the image of the hunting lodge depicted in the painting behind the chair flashed through his mind—of course!

The old hunting lodge, not used much anymore, certainly not this time of year—less than a mile from here.

How had he forgotten it? Had he been so zeroed in on the cave because of its relevance to Princess Analise's reason for her visit that he'd neglected to recall the lodge?

Fatigue gone, he popped to his feet and ran back toward the horses.

ANALISE STARTLED AWAKE with the sounds of Toby's cries echoing through her brain. Impossible. Nothing had changed. She must have been dreaming. Her stomach heaved with worry.

What if they'd killed Toby? What would she tell his parents? Tears took giant stinging bites in the back of her nose but she refused to allow them to fall.

There was something else at issue, as well, and that was the original reason for the visit to Wyoming. If Toby or she were killed there would be official inquiries as well as the attending media circus. For that matter, it might already be too late. Kidnapping was a federal offense. Her mother's reason for sending Analise to the Open Sky Ranch would come out and the information Analise was sent to secure and destroy could become public knowledge.

And that could mean the end of the Chatioux she knew and loved and the destruction of her family.

She couldn't let that happen.

Think. Do something to help yourself. Do it for your family.

The man called Doyle sat slumped in a big chair in front of the dwindling fire. Occasionally he lifted a bottle to his lips and drank, but now that she watched more carefully, she realized he wasn't even doing that much.

Was he asleep?

Hope surged through her at the thought. She

had to hurry. The other man might give up waiting for Pierce and return at any minute, but she couldn't sit here and waste an opportunity.

Think, Analise.

She could use the wall to push herself to her feet if she could just roll back into a sitting position without arousing Doyle's attention. She'd never done it that way before, but she'd seen her older brother, Alexander, do it on occasion. She devoted the next few minutes to getting situated, freezing every time the dry hay rustled beneath her weight. Finally she was ready to press her back and bound hands against the wood and, slivers be damned, push with her leg muscles. It was way harder than Alexander made it look....

Doyle made a snorting noise. His hand dropped to his side and the empty flask he'd been holding toppled harmlessly to the wood floor.

Where did he keep that knife? Where was the little gun he'd taken from her? Something, anything.

She would have to hop across the room. It seemed like a good way to commit suicide, but what were her options? Wait here like a lamb? She took a tentative hop, a tiny little thing a baby bunny wouldn't be proud of, but it gave her courage. Doyle didn't open an eye. In fact, it seemed his snoring became even more pronounced.

A few more modest hops began to give her

confidence. She would have to pass in front of the one big window that wasn't boarded up or hopelessly cracked and if Lucas happened to be watching, that would be dangerous, but there was no other choice.

She could see the pocket of Doyle's coat hanging down by his legs and it looked as though it held something relatively heavy. Like a knife. She kept at it, small hop after small hop, biting down hard on the gag as she moved, struggling to control her breathing.

Finally she was at his side. She would have to reach in at an angle because of the way her wrists were tied behind her back. The trick would be to move quickly but gently.

Fate favors the bold. That's what her father was fond of saying.

Turning, she bent her knees and slipped her hands into the deep pocket.

Her fingers touched steel. Not the knife. She'd hit pay dirt. The small gun slipped into her hands and for the first time since this ordeal began, she felt sure she could turn things around. Could she shoot this guy? Hell, yes.

Slowly, she pulled her hands and the precious gun from his pocket, working out in her head how she could get into a position where she could use it. But then a vise clamped onto her wrists and a second later, Doyle pulled her down across his lap. "Well, hi there, darlin'," he slurred.

Disappointment rose up her throat.

He pried the gun from her fingers and pointed it at her forehead. "This what you was going to do to me, darlin'?"

His finger squeezed the trigger and she flinched but although there was a clicking noise, it wasn't a bullet that appeared. Instead a small flame shot out the barrel.

A cigarette lighter? Her salvation was a cigarette lighter?

"Bet you wish you'd found this instead," he said, and this time he held the knife, the lethal-looking blade just inches from her face.

With a leering grin, he lowered the tip in slow motion. Analise lay as still as a terrified mouse trapped under a cat's paw as the broad blade filled her vision. The cold touch of metal grazed her cheek, and a second later, he'd cut the gag free and pulled it from her parched mouth.

"How about showing me a little gratitude?" he said, pawing at her. His plans for her were pretty damn clear.

She turned her face away and his damp lips connected with her ear. "You're a dead woman," he hissed.

Analise jerked away, half falling to the floor. Doyle swore at her but it was swallowed by a gunshot coming from outside. He instantly grabbed her hair and pulled her across the room. With one violent motion, he threw her on the hay, then lurched back to the fireplace for his gun, and this one wasn't a toy. Holding the knife in front of him, he shoved the gun in his belt. It had been on the hearth and she hadn't seen it.

To Analise, a gunshot meant rescue and rescue meant Pierce Westin. She lay on the hay, determined to help if she could.

Opportunity presented itself as Doyle raced toward the door. With all the strength fueled into her hatred of this man and her desire to be free, she rolled herself in front of him. He fell over the top of her, falling hard and fast on top of her. Right before she passed out, she heard an unholy sound issue from his mouth.

PIERCE LOOKED AT the lodge and the small barn from a distance. What would he do if he was the captor?

If alone, he'd stay in the house with the princess.

If there were two or more, he'd send someone to the barn loft for a good vantage point. Since Pierce wasn't sure who or how many he was looking for, it made sense to start with the loft.

The first good news he received came as he sneaked into the barn and found two Open Sky snowmobiles and the battered trailer used to haul gear around the ranch. There was an old tarp in the trailer and some blackened cord but nothing else—no bodies, hallelujah! Two snowmobiles meant at least two captors.

And it meant Analise was here.

It was getting dark by this time and the barn was deeply shadowed. A slender ladder led up to the loft. Pierce climbed it slowly, methodically, chafing with anxiety to just get it over with, tempering that anxiety with caution. He had no advantage except surprise. He couldn't afford to waste it.

He'd left his hat downstairs and he peered over the edge into the loft itself, certain at first that he'd figured things wrong. But then he heard a soft snore and gazing into the gloom, finally made out a figure huddled in a blanket in front of the partially open hay door.

Lucas.

Had he escaped or was he part of this?

Still aiming for stealth, Pierce hoisted himself into the loft and began a slow walk toward his hired hand. He saw the rifle in Lucas's hand and made sure his gun was in his own.

With less than ten feet to cover, Lucas awoke with a start. His gaze immediately swiveled around to Pierce. He tried to jump up but got tangled in the blanket and stumbled. Pierce rushed the last few feet, unwilling to shoot, but Lucas had no such compunction and a shot whizzed past Pierce's ear.

Now whoever was in the house would know someone was out here.

"Damn," he muttered even as caught Lucas around the waist and wrestled him to the floor, knocking the rifle out of his grip.

"You traitor, where is she?" he asked as he patted Lucas down and retrieved the rifle from the floor. "How many of you are there?"

Lucas glared at him.

Pierce nodded his head toward the ladder. "Let's go. And you better pray the princess is okay." Somehow, he got himself and Lucas down the ladder. "Put your hands on top of your head," he snapped as he shoved Lucas out the side door ahead of him.

The snow had started again, and it was clear it wasn't going to let up anytime soon. Maybe that and the encroaching night would help obscure him and Lucas marching toward the house, maybe it wouldn't.

There was a back door to the lodge but Pierce didn't want to take the time to use it, not when that wild bullet had sounded an alarm. He kept his gun trained on Lucas's head as he pushed him along.

"Did you kill Darrell?" he asked pointedly.

"I'm not saying anything."

"In case you haven't noticed, this isn't exactly a courtroom where you can plead the Fifth, you moron."

Lucas shook his head.

"You started the fire, didn't you?"

"Needed a diversion," he grumbled.

"You damn bastard. Call off whoever is in there with the princess."

"Or you'll what? Shoot me?"

"I might. Or maybe I'll just bash in your head and leave you to die like you did that defenseless little kid, or better yet, maybe I'll stuff you in an ice hole like you did Harley."

"Hey, now, wait just a second, I never hurt no one."

"Give it up, Lucas. You're a lousy liar."

"No, it's true. I didn't do any of that." Some of the bravado slipped from his voice.

"I'm listening."

Lucas shook his head.

"Talk," Pierce urged, his voice low. "If you didn't kill anyone, this is your big chance for redemption."

"Doyle," he muttered at last.

"Doyle? As in your brother? He's with the princess?"

Lucas nodded.

"He killed Harley and beat up the kid?"

"Yeah. I tried to stop him. The kid was scream-ing and kicking...."

"I bet you tried."

"Doyle gets crazy when he drinks."

"I suppose he killed Darrell, too?"

Lucas hunkered into his coat and didn't re-spond.

"Who else?" he prompted.

"Who else what?"

"Who put you and Doyle up to this? Was Harley involved? Did you guys have an argu-ment?"

"I ain't saying no more. You know about Doyle, that's enough."

He was right; Doyle was the problem right now. "Call him off," he demanded. "Right now, or, so help me, I'll shoot you in the foot and work my way up." He made his point by jabbing the barrel of the gun against Lucas's boot.

"Doyle! Come on out," Lucas called. "Bring the girl."

"Louder," Pierce coaxed with a jab.

Lucas repeated himself. There was no re-sponse.

The Doyle Garvey Pierce remembered wasn't a man of finesse. If he was in that house with the princess he'd be marching her through the door threatening to kill her or at the very least firing shots through one of the cracked windows.

"Let's go," Pierce said, and shoved Lucas ahead of him again, pulling him upright when he slipped. As they stepped onto the porch, Pierce glanced through the big window, but it was even darker in there than outside. And then he saw a dark heap on the floor.

He shoved Lucas against the side of the house and tried the knob. It opened readily.

"Analise?"

He was greeted with silence. The heap didn't move. His heart froze.

"Get in here," he said, turning back to Lucas, just in time to hear the second shot of the day. Instinctively dodging out of the way, he looked back for Lucas who was sliding down the outside wall, bullet hole in his forehead, eyes open and surprised-looking. Half of the back of his head was gone.

For a second, Pierce was dumbstruck. Who in the hell had fired that shot? He looked across at the barn from where the shot had to have come, but it was too dark to see. Self-preservation finally kicked in and he scrambled into the lodge, slamming the door behind him.

Chapter Fifteen

Analise came to as a heavy weight lifted from her chest. Her eyes flew open. A scream died on her lips as the shadowy figure looming over her turned into a familiar one.

"Pierce!"

"I thought you were dead," he said, and then she was in his arms, tears she'd fought for so long running freely down her face.

He held on to her as though she was a mirage and he was afraid if he let go she'd disappear. The image came easily as it was exactly the way she held on to him.

And then he was leaning back and she knew he was trying to see her through the dim light and she knew it didn't matter if they were blurs to each other. In the next instant, he'd pulled her back against him and cupping her face in his hands, kissed her lips.

His face was rough with stubble and cold from the snow and it felt wonderful against her skin, he felt real, and his kiss was the fabric of fantasy. Happiness welled inside her like an untamed artisanal well, tickling her from the inside out with the delirious feeling of safety she'd thought she'd never again experience.

Toby!

"Where is he?" she cried, looking deep into Pierce's eyes. "Pierce, where is he?"

He helped her to her feet. "He's dead. He must have fallen on his knife."

"Not Doyle," she whispered, almost afraid now to hear it. "Toby. Where is Toby?"

Pierce's handsome face grew solemn. "They bashed him on the head. There was some kind of horrible fight—"

"At the ice shack," she muttered.

"That's right."

"Was Harley one of them?"

"I think so. Something must have gone wrong at the ice shack, though, because he was dead when I found him."

"And Toby? How badly is he injured?"

"No way to know. Jamie took him back to the ranch. They'll move heaven and earth to get him to a doctor."

"Don't you have a cell? Can't we try to reach the ranch or Jamie? I have to know about Toby—"

"In a minute. I have to go outside and check

the barn. Someone killed Lucas a few minutes ago. They may still be out there. I want you to stay in the house, lock the doors, stay away from the windows. Here, take Lucas's rifle. I'll be fast."

"Be careful," she said, kissing him again. Now that he was here, it was unbearable to let him go, even for a few minutes. "Come back to me," she said.

He kissed her forehead, then slipped through the front door into the night and was gone.

She stood with her back against the door, the gun in her hands although she wasn't sure how to use it. Five minutes passed in agonizing slowness then she heard Pierce's voice and a soft rap. "Analise?"

She opened the door and he came inside. She could barely see him in the darkness.

"I think we can risk light now," he said. "Whoever was here is gone. He took one of the snowmobiles and destroyed the other. I didn't even hear an engine."

Analise was just glad whoever it was had left.

Pierce produced a flashlight and together they found a few candles and lanterns and illuminated the room. Doyle's huge shape seemed to shrink as they worked and Analise did her best not to look at him.

"There's a lot to do," Pierce said.

"We have to call about Toby."

He dug the cell from a deep pocket. "We can try. I'm not promising anything. The signal lines are weak." He punched in a number and held it low so she could hear it ring on the other end.

"Pierce?"

"Jamie, thank goodness. The boy—"

"...doc...recovery."

"You're breaking up," Pierce said, with a swift look at Analise. "Are you saying the boy is out of danger?"

"No...danger," Jamie said.

"Jamie, listen. Is everyone at the ranch? I mean all of the princess's party, are they accounted for?"

"The ranch...fine," Jamie said.

"No, the people—"

"...princess?"

"Yes, I have her. She's safe. About the people—"

"The princess?" Jamie said again.

"Safe," Pierce repeated.

Silence. The signal was gone.

Pierce set the phone aside.

"It sounded as though Toby saw a doctor," Analise said, taking a deep breath. There had been no desperation in Jamie's voice.

"I'm sure Jamie will let the general know you're safe and the general can call your father."

"If he heard you tell him," she said. Then she

added, "My father will do what is best for Chatioux regardless of my fate. He would never give in to pressure like that."

"Even for you?"

"Especially for me. How are we going to get back?"

"I left two horses tied under some trees. I need to go get them into the barn and take care of—well, him." He nodded toward Doyle Garvey's body. "And Lucas, too, for that matter."

"And then we can go?"

"Not until daybreak. We can't wander around out there in a storm in the dark with a murderer loose."

AFTER DRAGGING BOTH dead men out to the barn and hefting them into the trailer where he covered them with the tarp, he went to find the horses. He settled them in two of the stalls and fed them some leftover hay he found in a third. Then he took a few minutes to jerry-rig traps over both doors. If anyone tried to tamper with the horses, a god-awful racket of falling tools and paint cans would bring him running.

Back on the lodge porch, he stripped off his gloves and coat and left his boots by the front door. He paused by the fire to warm his hands before collapsing on the sofa, and then had serious doubts he'd ever get up again.

The princess had been busy during his absence. She'd managed to start the old propane stove and had several big pots and kettles of water heating even as they spoke. She even handed him a warm, wet cloth which he ran over hands and face.

She hadn't told him how she came by the cut on her cheek and the bruise on her forehead, but he'd found a pocketknife on Doyle when he moved his body out to the barn. No use wasting anger on a dead man.

Especially when there was a much better diversion so close at hand. Analise Emille was like a mountain flower braving a blustery spring. It amazed him that she was also practical enough to haul snow inside to melt, wash down a table and figure out an ancient stove. Hard to picture a princess ever having to do much scullery work in the castle.

Well, wait now. Didn't Snow White do things like this? And Analise kind of looked like Snow White with her ebony hair and porcelain skin.

Okay, he was way beyond bushed.

"It seems to me I've been cold forever although I have to say Chatioux has much this same kind of winter," the princess said as she emptied the contents of the saddlebag he'd brought with him from the barn. Wrapped sandwiches, fruit, cookies—typical Pauline fare. It all looked delicious. "Everyone in my country skis," she added, casting him a smile.

"I have a hard time picturing General Kaare on skis," he told her.

"You'd be surprised. He was quite the athlete in his day and still practices. Even Bierta and Mr. Vaughn take to the slopes when we travel."

Hard to picture any of them on a vacation for some reason. Were one of them in on the kidnapping? Had one of them killed Darrell? He'd seen snowshoe tracks coming toward the barn when he searched for the horses—whoever had killed Lucas had apparently arrived in that manner.

"Lucas couldn't have killed your driver in Seattle," he mused. "He was at the ranch at the time, but Doyle might have traveled. What I can't see is either Garvey coming up with this plan on their own, especially since one of them told Bierta their goal was to stop your father's vote. Men like the Garveys do stupid things like this for one reason—money. They would have no interest in the internal workings of a country half a world away."

She perched on the edge of a chair facing him. "Or maybe they do stupid things for love," she said softly.

"What do you mean?"

"Doyle Garvey was teasing Lucas about a girl.

He said Lucas would have a chance with her now that he had money and Darrell was dead."

"Oh, God," Pierce groaned.

"Do you know who he meant?"

"Miley Lindquist."

"Yes, that's the name."

"Pauline mentioned her. Apparently she was going with Lucas but recently got engaged to Darrell. Lucas was the one who suggested Darrell join him as a guard. I wonder if he killed Darrell just to get him out of the way. Are you sure you only traveled with the Garvey brothers?"

"After leaving the ice shack I'm pretty sure, yes."

"When were you aware of Harley?"

"It's all still so fuzzy. I remember being abducted—they used Toby to get me to open my door. Then I awoke in a small cold building that I heard them call the ice fishing shack. Toby and I were dumped in a corner. I was blindfolded but I don't know if Toby was. There was a big fight. I heard Toby shouting. And Harley, too, but his voice sounded funny."

"Funny how? Excited? Angry?"

"I'm not sure."

"I found this in his hand," Pierce said, digging something from his pocket. He handed it to Analise. It was her diamond pendant, given to her on her eighteenth birthday by her mother. She hadn't realized it was missing, but now she recalled it snapping from around her neck.

"He must have ridden one of the snowmobiles. Maybe the Garvey boys shared the other."

She shook her head. Something wasn't quite right…

"Maybe there was a falling-out among thieves once they got to the ice shack and they whacked him. You can't remember anything before the shack?"

She stared at the sparkling diamond flower. "Nothing. I woke up at the shack and then again in the trailer after leaving the shack. I was alone by then. I found a gun—"

Pierce sat forward. "A gun? You found a gun?"

She looked around the room, obviously flustered. Spying what she was apparently looking for, she got to her feet and retrieved a small object from a dark corner. "I found this. I thought it was a gun but it turned out to be nothing but a cigarette lighter."

Pierce's brow wrinkled as he looked at it. "That's Harley's," he said at last. "I remember seeing him pocket it. From a distance, I thought it was real, too. And at the time I also thought it an odd choice of a weapon for a guy like him."

She ran her fingers over what passed for the grip. "His initials are engraved in the handle," she said softly. "BRH. I wonder what the *R* stood for." Her voice faded to a whisper and she frowned.

"Wait a second," Pierce said, quickly realigning what he thought he knew. "There's some charred, bloodstained cord out in the trailer. And Harley's wrist was burned. What if Lucas drugged him after the cookout and stuck him in that trailer, then added you and Toby later? Maybe while you were all being toted across the lake, Harley managed to burn off the ropes with his cigarette lighter. He could have attacked the Garvey boys at the ice shack."

"But why would they take him along if he wasn't involved?"

Pierce started to shrug, but stopped. "No one else witnessed Harley drinking or being drunk. I bet Lucas set it up to make Harley a scapegoat. I couldn't figure out why they'd bother to stop at the ice shack, but if Harley was making a fuss in the trailer, that might explain it."

"Lucas was furious with Doyle for losing control."

"I assume whoever killed Lucas did it to keep him from naming who hired them. I think he would have spilled his guts without much prodding. And if that someone didn't come with you then they followed me or already knew the destination." He yawned, and flashed her an embarrassed smile. "I guess I'm getting a little weary," he admitted.

"No wonder. It's been a pretty eventful two days." She handed him a wrapped sandwich. He sat there staring at it. He'd been so hungry but now all he wanted was sleep.

No, that's not all he wanted, he admitted to himself as he did his best not to stare at Analise. But his gaze kept wandering to her as she nibbled on a wedge of orange. To her lips, as succulent and juicy as the fruit. To her breasts pressed against blue cashmere. To her shapely legs.

"Aren't you hungry?" she asked.

He hadn't even unwrapped the food. "Not particularly," he admitted as their gazes locked and held.

She finally got to her feet and approached the old stove. As she hefted one of the kettles, he went to help her. "Let me get that."

"I have this one. Grab another."

He took what looked like the heaviest. "Where do you want it?" Until that moment, he'd been too tired to wonder why she was heating so much water.

"This way," she said, and led him into the bedroom. There were several bright quilts laid over the bed that he vaguely recalled as his mother's handiwork. "While you were out in the barn, I investigated the house."

There was a small adjoining room off to the left. As Pierce entered it, long ago memories of trips to the lodge flooded back.

In his day it had held two sets of bunk beds and was where he and his brothers spent the night when they went hunting with their father. Sometimes, way back before their mother took off, their uncle and his stepdaughter would come along, too. Even though she was younger than any of the Westin boys, she'd always insisted on a top bunk. Bossy little girl.

Echo, that was her name. He hadn't thought of her in eons. Soon after Pierce's mother left the ranch, his uncle Peter had moved Echo and her mother away from Wyoming, selling his share of the Open Sky to Pierce's father, and the two families had lost touch.

But now the room held little more than the cast-iron bathtub that had formerly been set up outside for extremely casual bathing. It was situated right smack in the middle like in an old Western movie. There were candles placed around the room and their light cast golden shadows.

"Dad must have parked the old tub in here after I moved away," he said. "Look at that, he even rigged a drain."

"I already wiped it out and put the plug in," Princess Analise said as she poured her kettle of water into the tub, steam billowing up around her lovely face.

After he added his, their eyes met. How was he going to get through the next hour knowing she was in here all stretched out in this big tub, naked and soapy and wet and did he mention naked?

He felt like gulping. Instead, his voice a little raspy, he whispered, "Enjoy your bath."

A smile curved her beautiful lips. "It's not for me. It's for us."

Chapter Sixteen

"Us," he repeated.

She looked up and away quickly. "Yes." She gestured at the only other furniture in the room, a small table which held a few items. "I even found clean towels and a sliver of bath soap."

"Do you mean us as in you first, me second?"

"No. I mean us as in, well, together."

He studied her. "You're a constant amazement to me, Analise."

"I am?"

"Hasn't anyone ever told you how unique you are?"

"I'm not unique," she protested.

"To hell you aren't."

Her eyes suddenly glistened. "If you don't want to—"

He stepped around the tub and pulled her into a warm embrace. "Want to? Are you kidding me? What man wouldn't want to?"

She buried her face against his chest. Her body

heaved with sobs. He smoothed her hair and closed his eyes. Damn, had Doyle—hurt her? He had to know. "Tell me what happened," he whispered. "Did Doyle do more than cut your face and bruise your throat?"

"It's not Doyle," she said finally, mopping at her eyes with the washcloth he'd snagged off the table and handed her. She cast him a look from beneath her lush lashes. "It's you."

"Me?"

"I thought I'd lost you," she mumbled. "I mean, I know that's dumb, you wouldn't even use my name. But now you say *Analise* with such tenderness." Another swift glance followed by, "Why is that?"

He wasn't sure what to say. Peering into her eyes didn't help. Every flip comment that occurred to him sounded hollow in light of her distress and what she'd been through and the misery he'd fought thinking of her all alone with those men. He heard himself mumble, "It's because I got to know you while I looked for you."

Her brow furrowed. "I don't understand. How could you get to know me when we were apart?"

"I got to know the you inside of me," he said, compounding the confusion he felt about everything and yet also sensing that he'd actually hit close to the truth. "I got to know the you in here," he added, and this time touched his chest over his heart. "The you that I'd spoken with and kissed and been afraid to want."

The tears dripped down her cheeks as she stared at him. "All I could think today," she said softly, "was that I was so sad I hadn't slept with you the night before this all happened. If I was going to die, then I was sorry I hadn't been with you just that once."

"You're a princess, Analise. You have a big future planned. You don't want to jeopardize it. God, am I really saying this?"

She put her lips against his ear. "For this one night I don't have to be a princess. For this one night maybe I could just be a woman."

He was so afraid he would miss something she said or misunderstand a nuance he all but stopped breathing. He still couldn't believe what he was hearing—

"I thought wanting you would go away when I saw you again, *if* I saw you again," she added. "But it didn't."

"Analise," he whispered, pulling her even closer. "You're all I can think about, too. I couldn't stand knowing how frightened you must be. When I saw Harley and Toby, I about died inside thinking you might suffer the same fate."

She slowly touched his mouth with hers, ran her tongue across his lower lip. "So you'll take a bath with me?"

"Of course," he muttered.

She stepped away and unbuttoned her blouse. It slid off her arms and onto the floor and he did everything but gasp with instant, flaming desire. Her jeans came next. She stood before him in skimpy silk underwear, as perfect a woman as he'd ever in his life seen and though it was too poorly lit to tell for sure, he imagined her cheeks were flushed the same pale pink as her bra.

"Your turn," she said.

He pulled off the flannel shirt and the T-shirt beneath, hoping the sudden flare of her eyes meant she appreciated him the same way he did her. She put a hand on his chest and ran cool fingers down toward his button fly. One more inch and he wouldn't make any promises…

She undid the first button and he took over because he could feel her hands trembling. Standing there in briefs that strained to keep him covered, he reached for her.

Her passionate response to their tongues entwining shot through him like a red-hot branding iron. He couldn't kiss her deep enough, fast enough. Her hands traveled across his back and up into his hair. He would gladly have inhaled her if he could have, absorbed her through his skin until there weren't two people standing together, but one. Her bra came off in one easy movement—the feel of her bare breasts pressed against him drove what little sanity he had left right out the window.

They were a runaway train. What was happening was going too fast for a bathtub. Still kissing her, he slid his arm beneath her ripe bottom and carried her into the bedroom. He sat down on the mattress, her in his lap, and kissed her again and again, his need for her swelling between them, until she stood up and slipped off her panties. She pulled him to his feet and guided his briefs down his legs, her lips grazing his sensitive flesh and raising the stakes. Reaching for her, kissing her, he gently laid her down on the quilt and wished it were covered with rose petals. She was far too beautiful for such modest surroundings....

For a moment he marveled at the ivory symmetry of her body that shone like a distant star in the dimly lit room, but she soon took his hands and pulled him down on top of her, pulled more quilts atop them, making a cocoon for two in the cold snowy night.

"Oh, Analise," he whispered against her ear. "I have to have you."

She answered him first with kisses, but then she cupped his face until he opened his eyes and gazed down into hers. "This can't change things with Ricard," she said softly. "I want you to understand that."

"I know," he murmured against her lips, teasing her legs apart with his fingers.

Again she responded like kindling touched with a lit match. He wanted to look at her, touch her, kiss and suck every little inch of her, but it wasn't going down like that. This wasn't going to be gentle and exploratory. From the beginning, he'd accepted the fact she was untouchable, unattainable and now to feel her naked skin burn with the same combustion as his own made his head reel.

"Come to me, come to me," she whispered urgently as he suckled each pink nipple. Her warm, eager hands guided him, her legs wrapped around his. He needed little encouragement. Her eyes closed as he penetrated her.

A small cry escaped her lips. Too late he realized he'd hurt her but when he tried to pull away, she caught his rear in her hands and pressed him closer. "Don't go," she whispered, her hips rising to meet his. "Stay with me."

As if he could leave. Her passionate cries echoed in his mind and in his heart as though filling all the cold empty places he'd almost forgotten existed.

Next time, tenderness, he promised her as they each surrendered to the other.

AFTER ADDING MORE hot water to the bath tub, they climbed in together, Pierce in the rear,

Analise in his arms, her back against his chest. During the time they'd spent in the bedroom, the candles had burned down even farther and the room was now intimate and remote.

"We should try to catch a little sleep before we go," Pierce said.

"Mmm," she said, trying to sound enthusiastic, but going back meant the end to this fantasy. Well, it had to end eventually. Although she was anxious to reassure her family of her safety and check on Toby and most important of all, complete her mission for her mother, she would have to reassume her old life. Trouble was, in the course of the past two days, she'd lost sight of exactly who that Analise was. Was that what love did? Did it shift things around deep inside? Did it change you?

How could she marry Ricard?

"Analise? You've gotten so quiet."

She wasn't sure how to answer so she snuggled closer to him. The hot water felt tepid next to the heat he generated inside her core. This was heaven, right here in this tub, in this man's arms. Baths would never be the same again.

She was getting maudlin. Enough of that. "I was thinking how much I love baths. My mother used to say she got wetter than I did when she bathed me as a baby because I splashed so much."

"I would have thought she'd have a servant supervise your bath," he said lazily.

"No, she was very hands-on with my brother and me. Giving a baby a bath can be fun, you know."

"I know," he said, his voice suddenly distant and she wanted to kick herself for reminding him of his son. "Patrick loved them," he added.

She was proud of him for staying with the memory of his baby. That took courage. "I bet he was adorable," she murmured.

"Yes, he was. He had a mind of his own, though. I used to think he'd grow up to be as stubborn as my father and older brother, but he never got the chance to grow up."

She wanted to ask him more about Patrick but she hated to pry. On the other hand, if she'd lost a child, she'd find comfort in sharing things, so she decided to take a chance. "Would it be too painful for you to tell me how he died?"

He laid his cheek against the top of her head. It took him a moment to respond. "Have you ever heard of SIDS? Do you know what it is?"

"Sudden Infant Death Syndrome."

"That's right. I was the one who found him that morning. The only positive thing was that he looked peaceful so it couldn't have been painful, at least that's what the doctor told us. He just…stopped living. I went into his room because he was late waking up. It was a Saturday and Erin was sleeping in. Patrick was just lying there, eyes closed, totally relaxed-looking, but I think I knew something was wrong way before I touched him."

"Oh, Pierce," she said, turning in his arms so she could see him. His eyes were dark pools in this light but the pain still showed. "I'm so terribly sorry."

His nod was almost imperceptible. "I picked him up and just stood there, holding him. I knew there was nothing that could bring him back, he'd been gone too long, he was cold, and...so I just held him. I think I thought it wouldn't be real until someone else knew. That's how Erin found us. She called the ambulance. I couldn't bear to turn him over to strangers."

Analise heard the catch in his voice and her heart ached for him. She kissed his shoulder, and laid her cheek against his muscular arm. "I think I understand," she said.

"It's been seven and a half years. He'd be about Toby's age."

"I'm sure he would have been a beautiful little boy."

"Yeah," Pierce said, and hugged her tighter. "He would have been great, but at least I had him for a year. It wasn't nearly long enough, not by a lifetime, but it was something."

They were silent for a while until Pierce spoke again.

"Analise, you had never made love before to-night, had you?"

"No."

"How old are you?"

"Twenty-six." She smiled as she added, "Oh, I can almost hear you thinking, 'How can a twenty-six-year-old woman be a virgin in this day and age?' Well, it wasn't easy, let me tell you. But my mother impressed on me how important it is to save yourself for your husband. How vital, really."

"Vital?"

"Wasn't it you who reminded me a little while ago that I am a princess?"

"Meaning there are stricter standards?"

"More or less. Besides, I've been informally betrothed for seven years. My fiancé is an important man in his own right with a very proud family. I've always known where my destiny lies." She paused for a second before softly adding, "Where it still lies."

"I've never heard anyone actually use the word *betrothed* before."

"It's old-fashioned, just like me. But in the years to come, at least I'll have this night to remember," she added, leaning back against him. She wouldn't add her next thought which was a repetition of what he'd said minutes earlier: It wasn't nearly long enough, not by a lifetime, but it was something.

"So, no regrets about having sex with me?"

"No regrets."

"Good. I have to say, for a beginner, you show real promise."

She laughed softly, but had to swallow a sudden sob and was glad he couldn't see her face, witness her tears. She loved the warm, solid feel of his nude body touching her back, his arousal hard against her tailbone, the way his hands linked under her breasts on top of her belly.

"So what will Ricard say when he realizes you've slept with another man?"

"Nothing," she said, knowing it was the truth. Ricard would not expect her to be as pure as the driven snow. He sure as heck wasn't. Purity wasn't the issue, but she wasn't going to go into that with Pierce.

"Yep, a continual source of amazement," he mused above her head, his voice soft and loving. *Soft and loving.* He was hers for this moment, but even if she wasn't bound to another man, there was no future for them, they were too different, they needed different things.

Was the love she felt right now enough to

compensate for the years of loneliness looming ahead? It would have to be.

His hands once again began exploring her body, creating a million sensations as they slipped over her wet skin. She closed her eyes.

"Now it's your turn," he whispered against the back of her neck. She turned her head to look at him. "Be mine one more time."

One more time, she thought as his kisses devoured her.

Chapter Seventeen

The snow had stopped during the night. Before the sun was up, Pierce got the horses saddled and ready to head back to the ranch. A few minutes later, Analise slipped into the barn, carrying his saddlebag. Her voice was soft when she spoke as though she was afraid someone was listening. While he strapped on the saddlebags, he saw her gaze dart over and over again to the trailer in which she'd been transported while drugged, gagged and bound.

"Are they under the tarp?" she whispered.

"Yeah. I'll lock the place up. They'll be safe here until the authorities can come get them."

She shuddered and looked away from the ominous mound.

The ride back was slow but it was also peaceful and gave Pierce lots of time to think. His mind raced through images from two decades before when he and his brothers had roamed this land on horseback, every ridge and hollow familiar, to a decade before when he was married and a father to a beautiful little boy, to a few hours before when he had buried himself in Analise Emille.

She sat astride the horse in front of him, a slender figure in the dim reflection of light off snow, a natural horsewoman. If she was flawed, he couldn't see it or bring it to mind. Everything about her appealed to everything in him.

And she belonged to another man...

It wasn't until daylight that the sun actually showed up for the first time in days. As its rays spread into the eastern sky, he realized he hadn't thought of Italy and Westin-Turner Enterprises once in the past several hours.

Bob Turner must be about ready to blow a gasket.

"I REALLY AM all right," Analise told her father and mother who were each on an extension of their phones. She pictured them sitting in separate rooms, her father in the castle office, seated at the huge desk that had been given to his great-grandfather by a Russian czar many years before. Alexander, thirty-eight now, married, his wife pregnant with their first child, would sit at that desk within months; he might even be a better king than her father.

Her mother would be in her suite overlooking

the mountains, much as the Westin den overlooked the Rockies. An attendant or secretary
was no doubt very close by, so her mother would
not reveal how tense she was. Analise could
hear it in her voice, though, and marveled that
her father could not. Analise suspected that the
twenty-year age difference between her parents
as well as their wildly divergent interests made
them a mystery to one another even after all this
time.

Don't be too judgmental, she chided herself.
*You're headed for the same sort of marriage to
the same sort of man....*

There was no way to tell her mother that she
hadn't yet had a chance to complete her search
as her father must never get wind that there was
one.

"Your aunt and uncle are on their way to Wyoming to meet with Toby's doctors, but I heard
from them a while ago. The boy is expected to
make a complete recovery," her mother said. "In
fact, I gather he awoke during the air transport
and was quite vocal about your safety."

"I'll call and reassure him," Analise said. "It's
been a nightmare here. The police are finally
on the ranch questioning everyone. General
Kaare and Mr. Vaughn are acting pretty darn
haughty and my new maid is in bed where she's
been since the kidnappers whacked her on the

head. The blow apparently started a string of migraines."

"Oh, my."

"She's agreed to see a doctor tomorrow. Anyway, the police are still here. It's not only my kidnapping and Toby's injuries, but the deaths of three other men in Wyoming and the possible murder of the driver in Seattle. I'm not sure when we'll get out of here."

"Has the press shown up yet?" her mother asked with a quiver in her voice. She was not publicity-shy; she'd long ago explained to Analise that it was the price for the privileged life they led, but this was different. All they needed was some enterprising reporter trying to figure out why Analise was in Wyoming. A connection between the queen and Pierce's absent mother would inevitably be uncovered and from there—

Analise couldn't bear thinking about it.

"Not yet," she said.

"Stay as long as you must, then come home where you belong," her father said. "Despite what Mr. Vaughn perceives as possible environmental concerns, I intend to throw all my weight behind the pipeline proposal. If Chatioux does not take advantage of this situation, the bid will go to Russia and that will weaken our position even further."

"I think that's wise," Analise responded.

"From what I understand, there are safe ways to go about construction."

"We will just make sure it's done correctly. You have a good head on your shoulders, Analise. You've conducted yourself like a king's daughter."

She smiled into the receiver. Leave it to her father to admire grace under pressure.

"There's one more thing," she added. "It's very possible that one of the people traveling with me is connected with this situation in some way. You should assign someone to look into everyone's background."

"It's already being done. General Kaare suggested it when he called earlier."

They spoke for a few more minutes, then disconnected. Analise had tried to give her mother clues that there hadn't been an opportunity for "sightseeing" hoping she'd catch on that her mission was as yet undone, but she couldn't tell if her mother had caught them.

The next call was to the hospital where Toby had been taken late the night before. His grandmother from Canada answered, and much to Analise's relief, Toby was able to speak into the phone, as well.

"Did Jamie get the bad guys?" the child asked.

"Yes, he did. Those bad guys will never bother you again."

"I'm sorry I knocked on your door."

"That's okay," she assured him. "Everything turned out fine except for poor Mr. Harley."

"I think his head exploded," Toby said with a small sob. Analise heard his grandmother soothing him, but Toby was determined to finish. "Mr. Harley was trying to grab you away from the mean one."

"We thought maybe he was," Analise said. "He was very brave. And so were you."

As she replaced the receiver, she noticed the painting behind the desk. It was of the house where she'd been taken, she was sure of it. The painting depicted the building as it would appear in the summer with the aspen trees leafed out and the grass tall with wildflowers, but it was the same place.

She felt no revulsion looking at it. The frightening time she'd spent there with the Garvey brothers had been mitigated by the subsequent time she'd spent there with Pierce. She stood up and touched the canvas, the dried oils ridged beneath her fingertips. She studied it hard, memorizing the details.

"Recognize the old lodge?" Pierce said from the doorway.

She dropped her hand and turned. "Yes."

He moved toward her slowly. She loved the way he walked, halfway between a cowboy and a city boy. Even running on half empty as she knew he must be, an aura of male energy propelled him.

For the life of her, she could not remember ever noticing how Ricard walked.

"It looks different somehow," he said, coming to a halt beside her. "I suppose that's because of what we shared there."

"I agree. Who painted this? It's lovely."

"My brother Adam. He inherited all the creative genes from our mother though he doesn't remember a thing about her. In fact, of the three of us, he's the one most determined to pretend she never existed."

They were silent for a second although Analise was willing to wager Pierce was as aware of her as she was of him. At last he sighed. "I hope I never I have to go inside that place again. It just wouldn't be the same."

As he said this, he moved away toward the gun case in the corner. He ran his thumb over the brass combination lock.

"Is something wrong?" she asked, joining him.

"I thought a rifle was missing, but it's right there." He rubbed his neck and looked as fatigued as she felt. They hadn't gotten a lot of sleep. It had been way too intoxicating to spend a night naked in each other's arms....

"The police are finally gone but they'll be back

tomorrow and this time they want to talk to you and your maid. It's no secret that a man connected to you was killed in Seattle. This thing stinks of a conspiracy. One of your people is in deep, Analise."

"I know," she said. "I wish I knew which one. What about Darrell?"

"They're checking his cell-phone records and talking to Miley Lindquist. They didn't say much, but I got the feeling they're thinking along the same lines we are, that Lucas Garvey lured Darrell into that shed to kill him, hoping Miley would turn to him for comfort." He rubbed his forehead with his fingers. "Did you call your family?"

"Yes. They're all relieved, of course. And I spoke with Toby in hospital. He misses Jamie."

Pierce smiled.

She put a hand up to touch his face and he grasped it. He kissed her fingers and whispered, "I need you, Analise."

She nodded but looked down at her feet. Clearing her throat, she decided not to respond in kind. If she was back to being a king's daughter, than she'd better start acting like one and that meant acting like a queen's daughter, as well. "Pierce, please, I know you've been a little busy, but I got the feeling the other day that you might have an idea about the possible location of my mother's lost possession."

He released her hand. "The mysterious something that you have to destroy."

"Yes. It's terribly important and after tomorrow there may never be another chance."

"Listen," he told her, leaning in close. She touched her stomach as his warmth seeped inside her, desire for him flaring. "The place I was thinking of is an old Indian site. There's a cave there. It's on family land and we caretake it, have for many, many years because the tribe is extinct.

"The cave is obviously a possibility. We were taught not to mess with anything having to do with the native Americans, but it's a big cave and I know there are burials there as well as artifacts. My mother's clue for your mother was something about sleeping with the dead, right?"

"'Resting souls, high in the summer sky,'" she recited, a flicker of excitement getting past the sensory overload of his proximity. "Yes."

"I don't get the 'summer sky' part, that doesn't make sense, but the 'resting souls' fits."

"Where is this place?"

"Beyond the lodge where we spent last night."

"Is it hard to find?"

"Not if you know where to look."

"Will you take me?"

He studied her face for a second. "My father is already coming unglued at the way things have gone since I allowed 'you people' access."

"Well, you can't blame him for that," she admitted. "But I only have tomorrow—"

"The police are coming, remember? They gave you today but by tomorrow they'll be all over you, the ranch, the ice shanty, the lodge—they'll have talked to the Seattle police..."

"Then we have to go now."

"Now? We haven't slept in two days!"

"If we go to bed very early and get up at midnight, we could do it. Please, Pierce. This is so terribly important."

He studied her face for a moment, then pulled her against his chest.

She knew she shouldn't go to him. What they'd shared was over; it was back to business. But her protests died in her throat as she saw the longing in his eyes and knew it was in hers, as well.

His lips found hers.

"Ahem—"

They tore apart like a bomb had exploded between them. General Kaare and Mr. Vaughn stood at the doorway. While Vaughn's thin face registered little more than curiosity, the General's disgust was evident in the twist of his lips. "Princess Analise, I insist you come with us."

"She's not going anywhere without me tagging along," Pierce said, stepping in front of her.

The general's lips curled in a sneer. "Is that so? You're taking many liberties, Mr. Westin. Although we are grateful you rescued our princess, you should remember your place."

"My place is beside her as long as she is on this ranch," Pierce said calmly. "And you damn well know why."

"Are you insinuating you don't trust me?" Vaughn said, his hand flying to his chest.

Pierce nodded.

"Listen here," General Kaare said, his eyes burning. "I have known King Thomas for decades. We fought together as young men. I am his closest advisor and confidant which means he listens to me when I speak. Princess, we need to discuss arrangements for departing this hell hole as soon as is humanly possible."

Analise leveled a steady gaze at both men. While she wasn't worried about Vaughn, the general's words left her stomach in a knot. His threat was indirect but she understood it for what it was and yet for the life of her, she would not allow this man to manipulate her. "I think," she said, striving to keep her voice even, "that once again you are forgetting it is we who have brought mayhem to the Westin ranch, not the other way around."

Vaughn apparently felt the tension, as well. "The housekeeper has made soup," he announced. "We're all tired and grumpy. Maybe something hot—"

"I am not interested in soup," General Kaare growled, dismissing Vaughn. "If you will not listen to reason, Princess, than I shall spend what is left of this miserable day on my own." And with that he turned around and departed. They heard the front door slam a moment later.

Mr. Vaughn spread his hands in a vague gesture of embarrassment. "Perhaps I will ask the housekeeper to deliver my meal upstairs," he said, and nodding his head stiffly at Analise, left.

"I thought they'd never go," Pierce said, reaching for her.

"You don't understand," she muttered, sidestepping his grasp. "They saw us kissing. So all that talk about being my father's confidant was General Kaare's way of telling me that if I don't shape up he'll tattle on me."

"And then what will happen?"

She flicked her hair away from her forehead. "Oh, I don't know. Questions, I guess. In the middle of the rest of this mess, it's just a complication I don't need to take back to Chatioux. The paparazzi will have enough to write about as it is. I've been careless."

A flicker of annoyance crossed his features

as he stared down at her. "Okay, we'll do it your way. No more hands-on."

"That would be best," she said as a chunk of her heart fell into oblivion.

"But you will think about taking me to the cave, won't you? The pipeline isn't the only thing that could kill my country."

"Sure," he said. "I'll think about it."

Chapter Eighteen

Pauline joined them for an early dinner, the Lab curled up by her feet, but she was the only one. Bierta was still down with migraines, Vaughn had taken his supper in his room and General Kaare had not resurfaced after the incident in the den.

"Excuse me for saying this, Princess, but your traveling companions are some pieces of work. Oh, not the little maid, she's been quiet as a mouse, though I checked on her over and over again yesterday afraid she might be worse off than she let on, but those two men. They wouldn't stay upstairs, I didn't even know where they were half the time and the ranch was a disaster yesterday with everyone trying to get feed to the cows and fix the machines...

"Well, I guess what I'm getting at is I really think you should be more careful who you travel with in the future."

"I agree," Analise said, sparing Pierce a quick glance. He agreed, too.

The soup was fragrant and warm, filled with chicken and small tender dumplings. It had been one of Pierce's favorite meals when he was a kid and it touched him that Pauline remembered.

"I wish Pierce's father could have joined us," Analise said to Pauline as she spooned broth. "I feel terrible our coming here has been such a disaster for all of you on the ranch."

"Oh, honey, it's not your fault. It's a shame about your bodyguard, but if Lucas killed Darrell over Miley, then only the Garvey brothers were hurt and they did it to themselves if you follow my drift. Those Garvey boys. And to think, there's three more of them at home and their father who's the biggest crook of them all."

"They're going to be pretty upset that two of them died yesterday," Pierce said. "It won't occur to them that it was their own damn fault."

"That's true," Pauline said.

"I still feel responsible," the princess said quietly, "and I will make it a point to speak with Birch before we leave the Open Sky."

"You'll have to go to him, then," Pauline said. "His knee can't handle the icy conditions outside yet but he is making progress. I've been helping him walk around inside the cabin the last few days and he's making noise about coming outside as soon as the snow melts some."

"That'll be good for him," Pierce said. "It's weird having him so absent."

"It's been a really long winter," Pauline added. "And he's been lonely."

"He has you," Pierce commented.

She didn't respond directly. "Adam set him up on a laptop a while back. He enjoys getting emails. He got one yesterday from—"

"Tell me it was from Cody. Did he say when he's coming back?"

Shaking her head, Pauline slathered butter on a slice of bread, making little tsking sounds in her throat. "I swear, Pierce, it's like you don't want to be here. No, the email wasn't from Cody, it was from your uncle."

"Uncle Pete? I didn't think he kept in touch."

"Of course he keeps in touch. You'd know that if you lived here."

"Yeah, well, I don't. What did Uncle Pete have to say? I was just thinking about him and his stepdaughter—what's her name?—Echo. Bratty little kid."

"She *was* a handful," Pauline agreed, "but not as bad as you were. She's a designer or something now. They moved to California a few years ago. Pete's wife died and now Pete is talking about coming back to Wyoming. I wouldn't be half surprised if he wound up here. 'Course, you'll be gone, so it won't matter to you."

What was with her tonight? Why was she picking on him? He slid Analise a look and found her eyes half-closed.

Pauline's hand grazed his in a conciliatory gesture. "Don't pay attention to me," she said with a tight smile. "It's been a trying couple of days and your father is just a bear. He hates being sidelined by that knee, and now Cody is off somewhere and you're chomping at the bit to leave and calving season is only a few weeks away—it's just too much for him. Thank heavens Adam gets home next week. Then you can leave and put the ranch behind you."

He patted her hand. "Pauline, when you're born and raised on a ranch, you never really leave it. It's inside of you."

"Then why did you go?" she asked.

He shook his head. "Lots of reasons. But not because of you or my brothers. Life just called me away, that's all."

"We need you here, Pierce. Your father says no one can rope a cow like you can and no one was as good with the calves—"

"My father said those things about me?"

"Yes."

He shook his head again. "I don't believe it."

"He's not a man given to handing out compliments, you know that," she said.

"Yeah I know that." He finished his soup and pushed the bowl away. His insides were all jittery like a hive of bees were stinging him in a dozen little hidden places.

"I feel like leaving here sometimes, too," Pauline said softly. "Maybe I'm just jealous because you get to go off and do exciting things."

Again Pierce looked toward Analise to see how she was taking this conversation, but she was out of it, her head to the side now, her shoulders jerking occasionally as her eyes fluttered open and closed again.

"They'll be gone soon," Pierce muttered. "Back to Chatioux, back where they belong."

Pauline nodded toward Analise. "You better help the princess upstairs before she lands facedown in her soup."

ANALISE WOKE UP at midnight on the dot. Bierta had already been asleep when Analise drug herself into the room after dinner, a bottle of aspirin next to her bed. Later, when this all quieted down and they were safely on their way home, Analise vowed she'd find a way to make it up to Bierta.

Meanwhile, gentle snores were the only sounds coming from the maid.

Still half asleep, Analise untangled herself

from the blankets and dressed quickly, then made her way carefully toward the door, snagging her boots on the way. She slipped into the hall without arousing Bierta and closed the door quietly behind her.

"You're prompt, I'll say that," Pierce whispered from the shadows.

She almost leaped out of her skin. Clutching the general area over her heart, she shook her head at him as she leaned against the wall and pulled on her boots. Then she walked toward his tall, dark shape.

"What would you have done if I hadn't been out in the hall waiting for you?" he asked her as they tiptoed down the stairs.

"I don't know," she admitted, fully awake now. "I don't even know which room is yours."

Downstairs, he wrote out a note. When Analise questioned why he mentioned their destination by name, he looked straight into her eyes. "I'm putting this in one of the red cups. Only Pauline will notice it when she makes coffee, but we have to cover our tracks. We have to let someone know where we're going." He patted the left side of his chest. "It's the same reason I'm carrying the Smith & Wesson. There's still a murderer loose or are you forgetting Lucas Garvey?"

"I'm not forgetting," she said softly.

Grabbing hats, gloves and coats from the mudroom, they escaped outside, staying clear of the overhead yard lights.

It was the first time since Analise had landed in Wyoming that the night skies were clear. Walking under a million stars, their feet crunching the icy snow, it finally felt as big and beautiful here as she'd pictured it before coming. So free. Surely this was paradise in its way, or would be if things were different.

She glanced up at Pierce and wondered if he felt the tension as acutely as she did. Well, how could he? It wasn't his world they were trying to save....

For days now, her mission had taken a backseat to the more immediate crisis of kidnap and murder, but now it loomed in her mind as the ticking time bomb it really was. What if this was a wild goose chase and they didn't find her mother's things? What then?

Well, she'd be forced to leave empty-handed, hoping it had been destroyed years before or that Melissa Browning Westin had taken it with her when she left the ranch. However, the threat that it would all come out would remain, a continuing plague on her mother's peace of mind and a possible arrow in the heart of Chatioux.

"Where are we going?" she asked as they bypassed the building where they'd returned the snowmobiles after returning to the ranch.

"While you were snoozing, I called Italy and brought out my partner, then I loaded a snowmobile and moved it a half a mile or so away so we wouldn't alert anyone when we started the engine."

"You didn't get any sleep?"

"I caught a few hours. I'm fine. I'm accustomed to time changes and short nights. Don't worry about it."

"Why did you buy your partner out?" she asked as he held a gate open for her.

He closed it quietly behind them. "I think I mentioned he wants to move stateside and get married."

His voice held a derisive note that irritated her. "Which you've already done," she commented dryly.

He stopped walking and caught her upper arms. Staring down at her, the moonlight highlighting his face, he looked unbearably handsome; she hoped he was about to kiss her. "True," he said. "I have. I hear Bob's girl is hot to fix me up with one of her friends, though. What do you think? Should I go along with it? Might be fun."

"Oh, absolutely," she said. "Of course you should. Who knows? Maybe one of her friends will be the woman who tames the beast."

"I'm talking about dating, not marrying," he said gently.

"I know."

"Do you?"

"Yes, I do know. You've made your position on the matter abundantly clear. Not that you had to. It's not like I ever asked."

"As a matter of fact, you did ask. In fact, you have marriage on the brain."

Analise squared her shoulders. "Really, we should be attending to the business at hand."

"Yeah, which is what, exactly? What are you looking for, Princess?"

She shook her head. He was back to calling her *princess*. Probably for the best.

"I think it's something you should think about," he added, taking her hand and pulling her along.

"I know exactly what I'm looking for."

"Do you?" he said, glancing back over his shoulder at her.

"Certainly. My mother's—"

"I'm not talking about your mother," he snapped as the shape of a snowmobile materialized by a clump of trees ahead of them. "I'm talking about you."

Analise clamped her mouth shut.

THE MIDNIGHT RIDE was long and arduous and by the time two hours had passed, Pierce felt like he'd been thrown under a bus. He wasn't as young as he used to be.

They both got off the snowmobile gingerly, removing helmets and goggles and shaking out the kinks in their legs. They were at a higher elevation than when they'd started and though the sky was still clear and the stars close enough to touch, Pierce was surprised to find just how cold the wind was. He'd known there was a breeze by the difficulty of handling the machine, but its intensity amazed him.

He untied the gear he'd brought along. When he turned back to Analise, he found her staring at him while holding her hood around her face with both hands. Her beauty struck him as it did every time he looked at her, though he could barely discern her facial features in the moonlight. He didn't need to see them.

It appeared she was talking to him but it was hard to tell as her clattering teeth and the wind howling through the evergreens snatched away her words. He leaned in closer, something he'd vowed he would never do again. He didn't need any more memories of her. The ones he had would be trouble enough to get rid of.

"What now?" she said.

He spoke close to her face, resisting the urge to linger. "Now we climb. It's not far." He gestured up the face of the cliff at whose base they'd stopped. The cave was only twenty or so feet up a gentle incline.

Was he nuts to bring her here? No doubt about it. Downright certifiable.

Moonlight thankfully shone on the face of the mountain and reflected off the snow. He used the electric light only on rocky patches, keeping one hand on the rocks and the other on Analise. By the ease with which Analise kept up with him, it was obvious she was in fine shape.

Well, he already knew that, didn't he? Scroll through the ten thousand nude images of her and he could verify she was in top form. More information to forget.

The entrance, when they finally reached it, was as dark as pitch and covered with a rudimentary slab of nailed-together boards, something new since he'd been here last. It was latched but not locked and swung inward easily. They hurried out of the wind and snow. It was soon pitch-black but refreshingly quiet and much warmer.

There had been torches on the walls when he was a kid but he had no idea if they were still there so he turned on the flashlight right as Analise flicked on a small slender one of her own. He tried closing the door behind them though it caught on the snow that had tumbled in when they passed. The wind sent it yawning open.

The passage they entered was about eight feet

across and sure enough, the old kerosene torches were still in place. He took out a box of matches from his pocket and tried lighting one, surprised when a flame flared. Adam had always been interested in this cave, both from prospecting and historical aspects; apparently he kept the torches working.

Analise pulled back her hood, sweeping her ebony hair away from her face with a gesture both efficient and graceful.

"Tell me about this cave," she said. "It was a burial site for an Indian tribe?"

"Prehistoric Native Americans," Pierce said, purposely turning away from her. He lit another torch. The light flickered in the air from the doorway, but less so than the one closer to the entrance.

"Do you know which tribe?"

The cave floor began a descent. "No. The name is lost. My great-grandfather came across the site when he was prospecting and recognized it for what it was. He made it a point to find out who they were and if their people still existed. My grandfather took over stewardship after his father died, and then my father and uncle. Now Adam is involved."

"And no one outside of your family knows about it?"

"I wouldn't say that," Pierce said. "Locals must know, but as for outsiders, I think maybe you're it."

"I'm honored."

"Actually, Adam is lobbying to turn the site over to the university for excavation. He's convinced it needs to be formerly protected. My dad's not having any of that. If it was good enough for his grandfather, then it's good enough for him."

The rocks on the floor had been pushed aside, making the going easier. He lit another torch and glanced behind them. The passage looked eerie in the waving light. "There's a cavern just ahead. Additional tunnels branch away from it."

"What kind of prospecting did your relatives do?" she asked as they stepped into the promised cavern. He flashed the light toward the ceiling far overhead and it glittered off stalactites covered with ice crystals. A flash across the floor revealed their counterparts, sparkling stalagmites.

When Pierce had first seen the cavern as a small child, he'd thought it was the mouth of a monster, filled with jagged teeth just waiting to gnash him into little bits of flesh and bone. It still looked pretty damn scary in the dark.

"Gold, but not enough to make anyone rich. I should know, I spent a lot of time looking for a quick way to fame and fortune. What's that?" His light had just glinted off a large metal object.

"It looks like a cart of some kind," Analise said as they approached it.

"I don't remember this being here before. Maybe Cody is getting over his failed marriage by digging for gold. Now, watch where you step, the debris is deep in here."

But once again, the way seemed clearer than Pierce recalled, a virtual path with footsteps in the dirt that could have been made anytime in the past fifty years.

"What's in that direction?" Analise asked as she flashed her light to the left.

"Another passage. It leads to a fissure that goes deeper under the ground. My great-grandfather started digging there after he found the Indian site. I gather he glimpsed some precious metal buried with a body."

"Wait, he unwrapped one of the bodies?"

"Well, apparently, most of the cloth had already rotted away." He turned to his side and flashed the light ahead of him. "The passage out of here is plenty wide but it's kind of hidden behind an outcrop of rocks. There it is," he added as his light picked out a looming dark shape.

"If this ritual is the same as other recorded rituals, the dead person was wrapped in his own blankets and clothes very soon after death. The women did this. It was they who transported the body and deposited it in one of the many smaller fissures in the next cavern."

"What did the men do?" Analise asked. He could hear her slipping on the rocks and reached out a hand to steady her.

"They were busy burning his house and his possessions. At least that's what happened in documented cultures and this seems to fit the pattern. Maybe if it was excavated, people could figure out how it all happened. All I know is family legend has it my great-grandfather found relics included in the binding, personal or ceremonial objects, he wasn't sure which. He felt so bad about disturbing the place, he put it back exactly as it was and forbid anyone to talk about it or excavate it."

"So your father is simply respecting this long-ago edict," she said as they finally stepped into a wider tunnel with a smoother floor.

"I guess. That's Dad. Honor and duty." He paused for a second before adding, "Stuff that's right up your alley, Princess."

When he realized she'd stopped walking, he turned to face her, flashing the light briefly across her face.

"What's wrong?" he asked.

"That's what I was going to ask you."

"Nothing's wrong, everything is peachy keen," he said.

"You know that's not true," she insisted and she sounded irritated.

He narrowed his eyes. "I don't know—"

"I tried to warn you that making love would not change my situation," she said so softly it was little more than a whisper.

"This is all in your imagination, Princess."

"It's my imagination that you're calling me 'Princess' again instead of 'Analise' and baiting me with tales of other women?"

"Do I detect a little jealousy?"

"Of course not. I have no hold on you."

"Ditto."

She glared at him. "You told me to ask myself what I'm looking for in some grand metaphorical way. Well, turn the question around. What are you looking for?"

He shoved his free hand in his pocket and stared at her poorly lit face. He should say something.

She filled the silence. "You're right. I do honor duty and maybe in such a way as it seems silly to you. You live for the moment. You don't allow yourself to project forward because you can't control what lies ahead. But that kind of control is an illusion and it guts the essence of living."

He laughed, the sound too loud in this deep, dark place. "Me?" he said. "Me a control freak? Coming from you, that's rich."

"I am not a—"

"You most certainly are."

They stared at each other until he rubbed his forehead. "If I'm acting surly it's probably because I haven't really slept in days. I knew you were spoken for when I met you. I accepted that fact when I made love to you. Am I happy about it? No. But I've moved on."

"And now you're going to have a whole company to run by yourself."

"Yes."

"So let me ask you this. Are you going toward something or away from something else or do you even know?"

"I know exactly what I want."

"And that is to build a life that assures you'll never have the time or energy to create a family who loves and needs you?"

"Do you want to know what I really want?" he said, his voice low and his temper spent. He took a step toward her and she backed away until she hit the wall of the cave behind her. He looked down into her eyes and it was like falling into one of the cave's seemingly bottomless chasms.

"Let me tell you in no uncertain terms," he said. And then added, "Better yet, I'll show you."

Chapter Nineteen

It all happened so fast that later Pierce wouldn't be able to remember who had made the first move.

One second they were facing each other and the next they were locked together. His flashlight fell to the ground and rolled to the side. He didn't know where hers had gone, only that it was very dark and the only sounds were the ones they created.

Her kisses turned his blood to molten lava that coursed through his veins, engorged his groin, thrummed in his heart—blood on fire, scorching him, scarring him for life.

She did this to him. Brought out the insanity. He could feel her presence from across a room; having her in his arms drove him wild. And what was really intoxicating was that he had the same effect on her. He could feel it in the touch of her hands as she reached under his jacket.

He all but exploded when she rubbed her pelvis against his.

"Oh, Analise," he whispered urgently.

"Don't speak, just love me," she said, moaning. Her fingers slipped inside his pants. When he pushed aside her underwear he found moistness and it drove the fiery blood right into his brain.

He pulled her jeans down her legs. His came next and yet somehow the kissing never stopped, never wavered, her tongue and his were the same, intertwined.

He entered her with a ravenous need that ate him from the inside out, and when she finally threw her head back and cried out, it was as though she pulled the climax from him, as well.

For what seemed an eternity, they stood together, wrapped in each other's arms, his face buried in her hair, breathing ragged. But eventually, she moved, and he lifted his head, suddenly once again aware of their surroundings and a little astounded by what had happened.

She disengaged herself from his arms. He heard her adjusting her clothes as he did his, trying to put themselves back together again, much as victims struggle to create order after the chaos of a hurricane.

"Analise, I—"

"Oh, Pierce," she said, her lips brushing his

cheek. "Maybe now we can be friends again. Maybe now you won't be so angry with me."

He started to protest that he hadn't been angry. Frustrated, hell, yes. But angry? Maybe.

Leaning down, he scooped up the flashlight. He wanted to shine it on her face but he didn't. He wasn't sure he could bear to look at her ever again.

"We're both a mess," she said.

"I'm sure you look ravishing. You always look ravishing."

"I'm not talking about on the outside."

"Ah. Yeah, well, it's hard to argue that. You're betrothed to a man you don't love and I'm a confirmed bachelor who can't get enough of one woman."

She touched his face. "You shouldn't listen to me. What do I know about life? Everything I said about you is also true about me, maybe more so."

"What do we do about it?"

She was silent for several seconds, then she leaned in against his chest, her head tucked under his chin, her arms wrapped around his torso. There was resolve in her voice when she spoke. "We find my mother's possessions, I destroy them, and then we get on with our separate lives. What else can we do?"

The answer seemed pretty obvious to him. She could break off with this Ricard character and come live a vagabond life with him. He would make her so content she would never miss having children. And if her parents disowned her and refused to see her much as his father had turned away Pierce, then he would be enough for her.

He took a deep breath as the absurdity of this scenario sank in. Analise's country and family were as much a part of her as her silken hair and crystal-blue eyes.

"And if I rethought my position on marriage, what would happen then, Analise?"

She was silent for a long time. She finally said, "I don't know. It's not that easy."

"The thought of you spending your life with a man who doesn't adore you makes me sick inside."

"Pierce—"

"How would you feel if that's what was in store for me?"

It took her a moment to mumble, "Sick inside."

He gently pushed her away but at the last moment, caught her hand. "We're almost there. Stay close to me."

THE PASSION THAT had swept Analise into Pierce's arms and the glow that had warmed her heart once it was spent began to trickle away as they moved down the gloomy tunnel. It began to take twists and turns she barely noticed. For a few moments she had belonged to the man she loved, and maybe for the first time she realized how monumental that was.

Was it possible to fall in love with someone in three days? A week ago she would have said no. Now she suspected it was. Pierce Westin was in her heart and always would be even if she never saw him again after today.

How could she live with that? How could she marry Ricard when she'd given every part of herself that really mattered to another man?

Still lost in her thoughts, she bumped into Pierce as they rounded more rocks and came to a stop in front of another rustic wooden door with a crude latch. "It used to be locked," Pierce said as he slid the wooden bar out of the hasp. "I'm surprised Adam doesn't keep it secure now."

"It's so remote, what's the good of a lock?" she mused as he pushed on the door.

"Good point. Probably Adam's way of thinking, too."

Their flashlights illuminated another cavern, this one slightly smaller than the one they'd left behind. The sides were riddled with crevasses and fissures. More or less in the center was a scattered pile of large rocks and south of that, a deep rift.

"Watch your step," Pierce said.

She pulled up short and flashed her light into the rift. "Whoa, that thing looks deep."

"About a hundred feet. When Cody took calculus we dropped rocks into it and timed how long it took them to hit bottom."

Pierce shone the light on the wall closest to him and revealed a torch mounted in the rock. He lit three more at intervals around the cavern until weak light flickered against rock walls, danced across the jagged floor. On his way back to her side, he bent over and scooped something up, playing his light into one of the crevasses that ran straight into the wall.

Back at her side, he used the flashlight to reveal a scrap of woven cloth and a small rock.

The cloth looked old and rotted. The rock appeared to have been carved. "What are these things?"

"This is part of a blanket, I think, and the rock looks like a bannerstone."

She examined it closer. It had been carved to resemble a butterfly, more or less, with notches on the top and bottom. "What's a bannerstone?"

"It was used with an *atlatl,* a spear, as a kind of weight to make the spear go farther and with more force. It must have fallen from one of the wrappings which means someone's been tampering with the remains. It sure wasn't lying on the ground when I was a kid."

"One of your brothers?"

"That seems unlikely. But there's no way of knowing when this happened without talking to one of them or my father. It could have been years ago."

"Or it could have been recent," Analise whispered. If someone was digging around in this cave for artifacts, they could have come across the exact thing Analise was on a mission to destroy.

"You look spooked," he told her.

"I swear the air smells different here. I know it's my imagination and that these people died a long time ago, but it feels wrong to disturb this place."

"I know. My mother brought me here the first time I came. My father had showed it to her when they were first married. She said she found the cave kind of spiritually uplifting."

"Do you?"

"Not particularly. But there's no doubt she felt it a place of resting souls. This has to be where she told your mother she'd hidden the infamous 'it.'"

"But she also said, 'High in the summer sky,'" Analise added. "That makes no sense whatsoever."

"Let's just start looking."

Analise shined her light into a jagged crevasse.

Six or eight feet along, she saw a skull amid a jumble of other bones and debris on the floor. A small gasp escaped her lips and she moved away. The next two crevasses held much the same, although occasionally she spotted what looked like pieces of pottery or carved arrowheads and once the shimmer of gold. More direct light and a closer look revealed a crude carved rock bowl with the head of a man forming a sort of handle. The man faced away from the scoop of the bowl, and the crown of his head was covered with gold.

"Wait a second," she said at last, turning. "Can you picture your mother reaching into a small space where someone was buried to hide something else?"

Pierce was across the cavern but his voice carried. "No, I can't, you're right." He turned to face her. "I didn't think of it that way."

For a moment she just stared at him. He was a good twenty feet away and the poor light made him little more than a tall figure in shades of brown and gray until he smiled and the flash of white dazzled her. Good heavens, she loved him. Her whole body felt bathed in the glow of her feelings and it was all she could do to get her mind back on the job.

"Maybe she used one of the smaller fissures that start too far off the ground to be a practical place to bury a body," he said as she turned away. "How big is what we're looking for?"

This required facing him again. "It's a diary," she said, moving her hands to indicate something the size of a trade paperback. It was pointless to try to keep that from him when he was supposed to be helping her search and even more to the point, she trusted him, she always had. "How are we going to look up high?"

"I can think of only one way. You're going to have to sit on my shoulders. But wait just a second. We're doing this to retrieve a girlhood diary? That's what's so important?"

"Yes."

"What? Is she afraid some reporter will get a hold of it and reveal she had a torrid love affair when she was eighteen?"

He said it casually, jokingly. She laughed, but it must have come a few seconds too late or sounded phony because suddenly he was right in front of her. "Analise? Is that it?"

She met his gaze and knew she couldn't lie, not to him. To the rest of the world, yes, but not to him, not ever. "Yes," she said very softly.

"Is that so terrible? I mean, I know she's a queen now, but she wasn't then and it's not the old days where people judge as harshly as they used to, right?"

She shifted her weight and shook her head. "You don't understand."

"Tell me."

Analise turned and walked a few steps, torn between loyalty to her mother and her feelings for Pierce. She needed him on her side, she needed him to lift her to look in the crags, it was the only way to get high enough without going back for equipment and they didn't have time for that. She couldn't do it alone....

She walked back. "When I announced I was coming to America and flying right over Wyoming, my mother told me things she'd never told anyone in the world except your mother many years before."

"If she was so worried about this diary, why didn't she come back for it?"

"I don't know. Stuff happens, you know how it is. She entrusted it to your mother and then your mother left and mine was afraid to draw attention to herself—at any rate, that's just what happened."

"What did she tell you?"

"Years before she came back to the States to finish her last term and fell desperately in love with a married professor. To top it off, she was engaged to my father and about to get married. The affair was brief and ended poorly. She returned home, married my father, and then she discovered she was pregnant. Seven months later my brother was born. He was a very small baby and it was assumed he was early."

"So, your brother isn't your father's real son?"

She nodded, knowing the implications of that would hit him very quickly. "My mother begged me to find the diary. If it got into the wrong hands, well, any hands for that matter—"

"Wait a second. Then your brother isn't the heir to the throne?"

"No. And what no one else knows is that my father is ill and has been for some time. My brother will become king very soon. If it leaks out his blood is not really Emille blood, he will never be crowned and our country will suffer because of it."

"Wait," Pierce said, staring down at her. "Does this mean you're—"

"Don't say it."

"You're the legal heir."

He'd said it. She nodded.

"Queen Analise Emille. We really are worlds apart, aren't we? Well, no matter, you'd be a wonderful queen."

"I don't want to be queen." She turned away. The cavern suddenly seemed full of watchful eyes and heedful ears. They were speaking too loudly, too freely.

"But you would be great, Analise."

He'd clutched her shoulders and she leaned back against him, eyes closed for a moment. When she finally spoke, her voice was softer but she'd never meant any words more. "Alexander has been training to be king his entire life. He's studied and dedicated himself to this. He's a kind and diplomatic man and he has the heart of a king. He'll be able to rule Chatioux fairly and make the tough decisions that are necessary for our country to prosper. I don't have the head or the heart for ruling. My wants and needs are much more personal in nature."

"Marriage, children—"

"Yes, those, as well as broader concerns like social equality. But not government, not ruling, not closing myself away in a castle for the rest of my life."

Pierce turned her to face him. Tenderly smoothing a strand of hair from her face, he kept his voice soft, too. "Honor and duty, Analise. Isn't that what you said?"

"Yes. If there was no one else, I would do what was needed. But there is someone, my brother, Alexander."

He stared at her intently. "Okay, I think I get where you're coming from. But once you make the decision not to claim what is rightfully yours, then I assume there's no going back."

"There's something else you have to remember. My brother has no idea he's not an Emille by blood. His wife and children believe they know everything about him and thus themselves. My father has no idea his son is another man's child. Knowledge of this event would not only disrupt Chatioux, it would destroy my family. I will take this secret to my grave."

"Then so will I," Pierce said. "And since this threat wouldn't exist if my mother had destroyed everything when she was asked to do it, I'll make certain it's done."

For the better part of the next hour, they moved along the walls, Analise balanced on Pierce's shoulders. A sense of urgency made her movements quick. She found creepy crawly things and webs, but no diary.

"I need a break," Pierce called at last.

Avoiding the chasm that partially divided the floor of the cave, he sat on a big rock. Analise climbed off his shoulders and collapsed next to him. The rock on which they sat was actually part of a formation that resembled a throne which was kind of funny in a way. It was easily big enough for two people.

"I remember this place," he said suddenly, his arm reaching around Analise's waist. "This is the rock where I sat with my mother that time she brought me here. That's the south wall over there. I remember her telling me that."

"Your mother sounds like an interesting woman."

He nodded. "She was."

"Were your parents close?"

"Kind of. Jamie said my father worshipped her. I've heard tales that suggest she was an outrageous flirt. And then, there was the postcard and the man she'd been rumored to be seeing who also disappeared around the same time…"

"It must have been terrible for your father."

"It was rough for all of us."

Analise took her flashlight out of her parka pocket and shined it on the far wall. Melissa Browning Westin had sat on this rock and stared at that wall. For several minutes Analise aimed the flashlight over the rocks. There was a natural pattern there, not a real clear one, but something.

"What do you make of that?" she said.

By the way Pierce jerked when she spoke, she realized he'd fallen asleep against her shoulder. "Huh?"

"Do you see a pattern on that wall?"

He studied it in the light and shook his head, then glanced at his watch. "Analise, we have to get back. It's almost 5:00 a.m. and we still have to travel and who knows what the weather's doing up top. The police said bright and early. I promise you I'll come back here after you've gone and search every inch of this cavern. If I find what you're looking for, I'll destroy it. You have my word."

"I know you will," she said, but she knew she couldn't leave, not just yet. This was her one chance and she'd blown it. "Would your mother have come here alone when she brought the diary?"

"*If* she brought it here, *if* we're in the right place," he said, smothering a yawn. "Yeah, I can't quite see her sharing that with my dad."

"So how could she reach the places we just searched?"

"She might have been prepared and come with some kind of step stool."

At that second, something clicked in Analise's brain. "I know what that pattern is," she said, standing abruptly.

"I don't see anything."

She directed the light on the wall as she advanced. "Look. The fissure near the floor is very narrow."

"Too narrow to store a human body."

"Exactly. And then it rises up the wall and branches off."

"Like a tree. Okay, I see."

"Or like a stalk of corn. A stalk of corn, a summer crop, on the south wall which, if you consider the warmth of the season, your mother might have dubbed a summer sky."

"I don't know—"

"And unless I'm mistaken, the holes and crevices that look vaguely like ears of corn from a distance are spaced so that they make almost perfect foot- and handholds. Here, I'll show you."

Sticking the penlight between her teeth, Analise stuck a foot in the lowest opening and grabbed the one above and to the right of it. Back and forth, she climbed the "stalk" until she was fifteen feet off the ground.

"Be careful," Pierce called. "I can hardly see you up there."

With the penlight in her mouth, she couldn't answer. She knew she was onto something. At the top, in a crevice that began a few inches above the long one, she turned her head so the light could shine inside. It illuminated a plastic bag stuffed back as far as a human arm could reach.

This had to be it. Relief bubbled up her throat. The last foothold was slightly canted and she was able to lean into the cave face and hold on with one hand. She took the flashlight out of her mouth and laid it on the fissure floor, and then reaching past it and balancing herself, she snagged the plastic and felt the reassuring sharp edges of a small book.

Once it was in hand, what to do with it? She needed both hands to descend.

"Analise? Did you find something?"

"Yes, I think so," she said, carefully stuffing the bundle under her jacket and gingerly beginning the descent.

His hands clutched her calves when she was still five feet from the ground and he lifted her the last couple of feet. He set her on the ground and looked down at her. "Are you sure you have it?"

"We'll know in a minute."

The plastic slipped off easily to reveal a lapis-blue book with *My Diary* emblazoned in gold on the cover. She opened it and her mother's elegant handwriting filled the pages.

Oddly, she didn't want to read a word of it. She already knew more than she wished she knew. It was enough to just know the threat looming over them all was all but over. "I can't tell you what a relief this is," she said, gazing up at Pierce. "Let's take it back to the other cavern and burn it."

"Better you should just hand it over to me," a new voice said, and Analise and Pierce spun around as one.

Bierta stood ten feet away and she was holding a gun.

Chapter Twenty

Pierce realized immediately he'd been so caught up in the chase he'd forgotten to guard their backs. He'd neglected to figure out a way to check all the rocks outside the cave, all the hiding places. Damn.

"First, toss your weapon over here, Mr. Westin," Bierta said. Her voice sounded different, but that wasn't the only thing about the maid that had changed.

Once before Pierce had seen her without her glasses and then he'd thought she looked myopic and vulnerable. But now, with her brown hair pulled back in a high, tight ponytail and her eyes full of purpose, she looked sturdy and decidedly fierce.

Her gun was pointed at Analise. Pierce hadn't brought a rifle with them for the simple reason it was hard to carry on a snowmobile with a passenger. He took the hand gun from its underarm holster, and ignoring her warning to empty it of bullets, all but threw it at her. It clattered to the rocky ground behind her, but she didn't move. Not once did she take her eyes—or her gun—off of him.

"Now, then, give me the diary," she said.

"Bierta?" Analise gasped. "You're the one behind all this?"

"I want that diary." The maid took another step forward. Her shuffling gait had disappeared along with her glasses. She waved the gun in measured strokes. "Get out of the way, Mr. Westin."

Pierce stayed where he was, slightly in front of Analise, reviewing his options. Apparently what he was thinking showed on his face, for the next thing he knew, Bierta fired off her gun. The bullet hit the ground a few inches in front of his left foot. "If I had wanted to hit you, I would have," she said after the echoes died down. "Now give me the book."

Analise shouldered her way past Pierce. "How did you know about this diary?" she demanded.

Bierta's smile was no more than a smug lift of her upper lip. "I didn't, Princess, not until I overheard you telling Mr. Westin about it. Up until now you two have made a mess out of my mission, but this diary will fix all that. It will break Chatioux like a brittle stick in a way that even your kidnapping and death couldn't have."

For a moment, Pierce thought Analise might give Bierta the book. Instead she clamped the diary tighter than ever to her chest. "What mission? What are you talking about?"

"Stopping the pipeline, it has to be that," Pierce said.

"Of course," Bierta said, almost strutting, "I've been working on this for more than a year."

"You recruited Lucas and his brother?" Pierce said, wondering how in the world this woman could have met up with Doyle and Lucas Garvey.

"At a place called Clancy's in Woodwind, Wyoming, months ago, right after the castle announced a layover in Wyoming for the princess and right before I became her humble servant," she said, and her voice slipped easily into a Midwestern twang. "Doyle wasn't hard to convince. He was a greedy man with big appetites and a tiny brain. It didn't hurt that he liked crude women and hated the Westin family."

"You were never a victim of the kidnapping," Analise said. "You didn't suffer trauma or migraines or any of the rest."

Bierta scoffed. "Of course not."

"I understand the politics behind this," Analise said slowly, "but I don't understand how you could be so ruthless with Toby. He's never done you any harm. And poor Mr. Harley—"

Bierta's eyes hardened. "People like you, Princess, and your spoiled little cousin are blights on the world. As for the bodyguard—he was expendable."

"You think everyone is expendable," Analise fumed.

"The Doyle brothers were weak. Killing the bodyguard in the ice shed and the other man in the generator building, leaving their bodies so easily found—stupid! They had no discipline."

"And so you shot Lucas to keep him from talking," Analise said.

Pierce shook his head. "She couldn't have killed Lucas. She was the only one Pauline saw over and over again that day because Pauline was worried about her after the supposed head injury. Her alibi is the only one that sticks."

Bierta waved the gun toward the opening. "You're stalling. I assure you, there's no reason to. No one but me knows you're here." At this she withdrew the paper Pierce had folded into the red mug before they left the house hours before.

Pierce swore under his breath.

"Who are you working for?" Analise demanded. "The environmentalists are a ruthless group at times, but I can hardly believe they would resort to outright murder—"

"No, Princess, they would not have the stomach for such daring, you're right. Let's just say it's in my government's best interest that the pipeline not go through Chatioux. It would have been easier if your country had passed on the undertaking, but no matter, we will win it by default when your country is shamed into oblivion."

"Russia," Analise said. "I cannot believe they would sanction—wait, you're from some splinter group, aren't you?"

"True patriots may hide but they never disappear," Bierta said with fervor. "And Chatioux may vote to sanction the pipeline, but once this diary is made public, your country will be in shambles and the pipeline will go where it belongs. Now hand it over."

"No," Analise said, and shoved it back inside her coat. "You'll have to take it off my dead body. I can't believe you got through the security checks...."

"Bierta Gulden checked out perfectly because she was exactly what her records said she was, a modest Chatioux woman with impeccable references and years of experience in domestic service. Unfortunately for her, she met with an untimely death right after I claimed her identity. Much as you're about to do. Give me the diary or I'll shoot the man."

"Like the 'accident' that befell my Seattle driver?" Analise demanded.

The woman called Bierta smiled again.

"There's irony in that. I don't know who killed that man. Apparently, he had enemies of his own. The incident in Seattle was unrelated to my mission which began and will end in Wyoming. I just wrote a few notes insinuating it was directed at you to make you uneasy. To get you to run to your daddy for protection."

"But it didn't work that way, did it?" Analise said.

"Just keep in mind no one would have died if you had simply told the king to vote down the pipeline."

"Don't try to blame your devious behavior and its consequences on Analise," Pierce said in a low voice.

Analise shook her head. "It's okay. She's a fraud. Nothing she says can harm me."

Anger flashed in Bierta's eyes. "I'm a fraud? What about you, Princess?"

"Me?"

"You're the one who's going to marry a man she doesn't love, not me."

"Don't you dare compare us," Analise said, fists clenched at her sides. She even took a few angry steps toward Bierta.

Bierta smiled. "Why not? Are you afraid your noble intention to sacrifice yourself won't stand up to scrutiny?"

"I am nothing like you. You lie—"

"And you don't?" Bierta scoffed. "Your whole life is a lie. Oh, yes, I've been following you long enough to know what Pierce Westin means to you. And yet you would leave him to marry another man."

"She's right," Pierce said. He'd just sensed a possible way out of this. Bierta was enjoying this banter with Analise to the point she seemed to have forgotten all about the diary. She was distracted....

Analise, predictably, turned on him. "You're taking her side?"

"You don't love Ricard. You love me." He grabbed her shoulders and steered her around to face the light as though trying to see her face better. This put them almost a foot closer to Bierta.

"You love me," he repeated. "You're willing to break my heart, and for what?"

"For her country," Bierta said with a trace of grudging admiration.

"I don't want to live like a nomad," Analise said, looking up at him.

"Then I'll throw away my suitcase."

"But you just bought out your partner."

"I'll un-buy him out. Unitex can have Westin-Turner. We'll both be rich."

"I don't care about money."

"I know you don't. Besides, we'll live in your

castle. I'll clean the moat, whatever you want, just marry me."

"For heaven's sake, Pierce—"

"Wait just a second," he interrupted and he stepped toward her which meant she backed toward Bierta. *Closer and closer...* "Aren't you the one who said I was running from marriage? Here you have a legitimate proposal made in front of a witness and yet you resist."

"I want children," she said, glancing up at him.

"I know you do. I know exactly what you want and what you need, and I wouldn't offer my hand to you if I wasn't prepared to meet those needs."

It was deathly quiet. All three of them seemed caught up in this little farce.

"No castle," Analise said suddenly.

"What?"

"Wyoming. Here, on the Open Sky."

"Here?" Bierta said. "Why here?"

Analise looked over her shoulder at Bierta as she spoke. "I could be happy here. I could be *free* here. And more important," she added, gazing back at Pierce, "You could be happy here, too. If you gave yourself a chance. If a wife and family is really what you want."

"I do," he said, and damn if it didn't sound like a vow.

Bierta's laugh sliced through the moment. "Isn't this touching? Doomed lovers pretending a future. Okay, I've been as patient with you two as I'm going to be. If you won't give me the diary I will force you both into that pit. Sooner or later, the diary will be found with your bodies and by then I'll be someone else. And if you don't jump, then I'll use your gun, Mr. Westin, to kill your bride and then you. A murder/suicide. The media will make you both infamous."

It was now or never. He raised his hands as though to plead, pretended to stumble on the uneven ground and instead launched his six-plus feet directly at Bierta's gun arm, figuring even if he took a bullet it would give Analise time to escape.

The weapon flew out of Bierta's hand as he knocked her arm down with all his force. But the woman was quick and strong, and before he could rebound from the momentum of his launch, she'd come at him with both hands raised. She hit him with a karate chop that sent him flat to his back, knocking the air out of his lungs, banging his head against the rocks. For a second, he was dazed.

Analise's voice brought him around and he struggled to sit up, unsure how long he'd been out. He found Bierta holding Analise by one arm, a gun pointed at her temple. Not just any gun, either. His Smith & Wesson!

Analise looked beyond fear, eyes as dark and

deep as the orifice into which she was careening as she clawed at Bierta. "Who else is involved in this?" she demanded. "Tell me!"

He staggered to his feet as quietly as he could, scanning the heavily shadowed rock floor for Bierta's gun. With her muzzle pointed at Analise's forehead there was no way he could chance another rush. She might have time to shove Analise to her death or shoot her.

"No more talking," Bierta hissed as she pulled Analise toward the rift.

He saw what he took to be the gun over by one of the fissures. He hurried toward it, gripping his head in a vain attempt to stop it from spinning.

"Bierta, or whoever you really are, tell me who's in this with you," Analise insisted, her voice commanding.

His fingers grasped what appeared to be the grip of Bierta's gun. Too late he recognized it for what it was—a fragment of human skull stained by the earth. He dropped it quickly as he caught movement from the corner of his eye and spun around so fast he fell against the fissure wall.

"I know you're over there," Bierta said, swiveling the gun to point at him as she shoved Analise toward the chasm. "You don't want your true love to die alone, now, do you?"

A shot bellowed as Analise, propelled forward by Bierta's arm, disappeared into the rift.

ONE MOMENT ANALISE was fighting to give Pierce time to come after Bierta and the next, gunfire and crumbling rocks sent her flying into the abyss.

Desperately clutching the chasm lip while her legs dangled over the chasm, she tried to find a foothold. She could do this. She had to do it. She'd seen Pierce collapse at the same time Bierta released her iron grip on Analise's arm. Had Bierta's gun gone off? It must have. Analise was almost positive Pierce had been hit.

She had to get to him.

But her fingers kept slipping and the muscles in her shoulders and arms, still stressed from being bound for hours the day before, once again set up a cacophony of protests as she fought to support her weight. She gasped out loud as the toe of one boot found a perch on an obtrusion in the wall, and she tried to use it to brace herself. She kept slipping.

The sound of running footsteps thundered in her ears. Someone was yelling. Had Bierta come to step on her vulnerable fingers? A shower of loose rocks rained down on her head, but then she felt the solid grip of hands clamping onto hers, grunts of exertion, and then the relief of being pulled slowly upward, her face ground into the side of the chasm as she struggled to help by using her feet.

At last the grip slipped under her arms and with a final yank, more than half of her body lay on the cavern floor. She heaved her legs over the side and took a deep breath, then rolled onto her feet, expectation making her pulse jump. Pierce had to be okay if he'd pulled her to safety.

Brushing tangled hair away from her scratched face, she could hardly believe her eyes. "General Kaare?"

He looked almost sick, his skin pasty in the subdued light, his tall figure stooped. "Princess Analise, are you all right?" She noticed his hands shaking as he patted her down in an uncharacteristically familiar manner.

She looked past his concerned face to the two dark heaps on the cavern floor, separated by only twelve feet. His gaze followed hers.

"Stay here," he commanded, picking up a rifle and looping the strap over his shoulder.

"I need to go to Pierce—"

"Please, let me do that. Please, Your Highness."

Pierce's still shape spoke to her in a million silent ways, robbing her of the ability to move. She nodded as tears ran down her cheeks, her gaze never leaving Pierce.

The general knelt beside Pierce. With each moment of utter silence, a little piece of hope died within her. When at last he stood, he looked back at her and shook his head.

Analise clutched her stomach and bent over. As the general moved off toward Bierta, she finally surmounted the cold grip of fear that had cemented her in place. She stumbled toward Pierce, barley able to see through a flood of tears, unable to believe he was gone. It had to be a mistake.

The general caught her arms. "Bierta is dead, too."

"I don't care about that woman," Analise mumbled. "Pierce—"

"Don't look at him," the general cautioned. He shook her a little. "Analise, listen to me! She must have shot at him the same second I shot at her. Her bullet got him in the face. He wouldn't want that to be your last memory of him."

"I have to see him. I have to—"

"Please, Princess. There may still be danger. I brought a snowmobile. We need to get you and that diary out of this cave. We need to destroy it. Think about your family."

The diary! She'd all but forgotten it. She grabbed her midsection and was relieved to feel the book still under her jacket, caught in the elastic band at the hip. She had to burn it. She had to save Chatioux from ruin. Something good had to come from all this tragedy.

Kaare's arm snaked around her shoulders. With one last longing look toward Pierce's body, Analise let the general lead her away.

Chapter Twenty-One

The long passage between caverns was dark except for the light from the general's flashlight. Analise recognized the spot where she and Pierce had stopped to trade accusations and then had succumbed to their feelings for each other. The light briefly illuminated the scuffle marks in the dirt that attested to their rush to make love.

He had loved her....

Her heart was a stone now, and it sat heavy in her chest.

How had she ever convinced herself she could return to Chatioux and marry Ricard and bear his children and that it was the right thing to do? It seemed impossible she could have been so naive. This had to be the very essence of bittersweet—to finally understand what was important right on the heels of losing it forever.

"How did you get here?" she asked, tearing her gaze away from an imprint of Pierce's boot in the dirt next to one of her own.

"I told you, a snowmobile."

They rounded the rocky outcropping and were swallowed by darkness except for the one light the general shone in front of their feet. "But how did you know to come *here?*"

"I happened to glance out my window and saw Bierta stealing across the field so I followed her. I knew either she or Vaughn had to be involved and it was hard to picture him actually *doing* anything risky."

"And the diary?" she added, sliding her fingers over the embossed cover. Her mother's secrets had led Analise here, to this place and this time. It had cost many people their lives, including Pierce. She wished the earth would open up and swallow the damn book—and her.

"I heard you talking to Bierta. I put two and two together." He was walking briskly. When his light illuminated a shallow basin in a rock, she grabbed his arm.

"Stop," she said. "We'll burn the diary right here. I don't want to take it outside this cave. I have a lighter in my pocket."

"As you wish." He knelt, propping the rifle against a small stalagmite. "Princess? I know how upset you are, how difficult this is for you. Hand me the book."

She put it in his hands, glad to be rid of it. History needed to die right now. He took it gently and she patted her pockets for Harley's novelty lighter which she found easily.

That's when she realized the general was thumbing through the pages of the diary, reading the passages with the help of the flashlight.

"Don't read that," she said firmly. "Here, give it to me, I'll burn it."

He looked up at her. "I remember these years," he said softly. "Your father was convinced your mother was the only woman he would ever love. But I suspected she was carrying on with a married man in America. I could never prove it, and here it is in black and white."

"General Kaare, please, don't tell me anything else. Just give me the book."

He didn't seem to hear her. "Your father wouldn't listen to my suspicions, refused to even hear them. He 'suggested' I join the military and then he made sure I was assigned abroad for the next thirty years. I was as good as in exile."

"But you're long-standing friends—"

"'A king has no friends.' That's what your father told me once. He was an egotist then, putting his own desires ahead of his country's, and he's one now, refusing to acknowledge the mistakes he's made."

Analise, taken aback by the bitterness in his voice, knelt down next to him. "You're talking about my father, your good friend," she said softly, prickles biting her skin like a horde of tiny gnats. "The past is over."

His face appeared a mask as he met her gaze. "Is it? Perhaps not." He slipped the book into his jacket pocket and stood up.

"What are you—"

"You've given me the means to revenge," he said. "I was willing to allow Chatioux to founder on your father's watch. Bierta convinced me she could ruin our chances for that pipeline and it would have served your father right. But this diary, this is a treasure. How far will your father go to protect himself and your brother? I intend to find out."

Trembling anew, Analise rose, too. "You know he's dying," she said. "What will torturing him now accomplish?"

He shook his head. "You can't begin to understand how much I loathe the man," Kaare said. "And your brother is just like him, full of himself." Kaare threw back his head and laughed. The sound was dry and hollow. "And to think the boy is nothing but a schoolteacher's son. That means you're in line for the throne, you'll be queen. It will tear them all apart."

"Give me that diary," Analise insisted.

"You aren't queen yet," the general said. "Come to think of it, Princess, I don't think you should return to Chatioux. With you dead, perhaps the king will see reason and do what is right for Chatioux."

"Which is what?"

"If I save the country, I see no reason why I shouldn't rule it. Your father has enough life left in him to pave the way for me. I'm sorry, dear, but you're in my way."

He was standing between her and the outside. The cavern around them was pitch-black except for the one small pool of light at Kaare's feet. As he reached for the rifle, she knocked the flashlight to the ground and heard the satisfying shatter of glass. She took off the way they'd come, stumbling over rocks, afraid to look back, bumping into stalagmites, skinning her legs right through the denim.

"You can't get away, Princess. I don't need a flashlight. I have a night-vision scope," Kaare called out after her. "How do you think I killed Lucas Garvey?" A shot rang out and hit something nearby.

She found the outcropping by sheer luck and ducked around into the tunnel, running for her life on more even ground.

Until she ran into something solid.

PIERCE KNEW WHO it was, even in the dark.

Especially in the dark.

He flashed on the light just to reassure her

though he knew the bloody condition of his face and clothes might scare her instead. With realizing it was him, her eyes went from terrified to incredulous. "Oh, my God," she said, hugging him tightly. "I thought you were dead!"

And then she snatched the light away from him and turned it off. "He's after me," she whispered, tugging Pierce back toward the burial cavern. "He has a scope...."

He didn't have to ask her who—he knew. He also knew the rifle and the damn scope—they belonged to Cody. General Kaare must have heard the location of the gun-case combination when Pierce told Pauline where to find it.

"He killed Lucas," Analise whispered as they hurried in the dark.

That's what he'd noticed in the case the night before. Kaare must have taken the weapon when he came after them in the snow, killed Lucas, then returned the weapon to its case. He'd left the scope attached and it hadn't been before but Pierce had been too exhausted to figure out what was different....

Analise's hand in his was cold to the touch. "I thought you were dead," she said.

"I pretended," Pierce said. He'd probably looked dead after Bierta's bullet grazed his forehead and scalp. He'd heard Kaare coming, opened one eye and seen the rifle and the scope and everything had suddenly made sense. Kaare had killed Lucas, he was Bierta's accomplice, he'd killed Bierta just as he'd killed Lucas, to protect himself. He and Bierta must have gotten here on the snowmobile Kaare stole from the lodge barn the night before because all the others were locked up. He must have left it somewhere undercover....

After Kaare talked Analise into leaving, Pierce had crawled around and found Bierta's revolver and it was a nice, heavy weight in his belt right now.

"Hurry," he said unnecessarily. They were both flying, feet barely touching the ground.

They wended their way through the boulders at the door of the burial cavern and reentered the chamber.

"I have an idea," he said quickly as they circumvented the chasm. Actually he had two, but he discarded the one that required him to play dead a second time. The fissure where he'd originally fallen was hemmed in by rocks with no clear sight of the cavern opening. "Sit on the rock, the one that looks like a throne," he told her, shoving the flashlight into her hands. "When you see him coming, shine the light straight at him, you understand, right at his face."

"Yes, yes," she mumbled, veering off toward

the rocks. He was asking her to be the bait. She had to know that.

He ran past her to the southern wall and started climbing until he was at the top of the "corn stalk." It was very dark up here, Analise's little flashlight having burned out. He retrieved the gun out of his waistband and balanced himself. Just in time, too.

The general appeared in the entrance at a ninety-degree angle to Analise. She raised the light, suddenly illuminating Kaare like a hapless actor caught in stage lights. The general immediately lowered his weapon, blinded by the infrared night scope.

There was time for one shot. Pierce aimed and fired.

The general sank to the ground.

THEY LEFT KAARE where he fell dead although Pierce took the diary out of the general's pocket. Analise turned her head, unable to watch.

Holding hands, she and Pierce made their way back to the main cave and set the diary aflame, sitting around it like some kind of macabre campers, waiting until every last page was reduced to ashes. Those Pierce scooped up in his hat.

The air outside was cold and dark, the moon descending into the west. Stars Analise had been certain neither of them would ever see again twinkled right as they had forever and ever; the wind still moved the tops of the towering trees.

Analise took Pierce's hat and held it so that the wind caught and scattered the ashes. When they were all gone, she looked up at him. "I knew what you were doing in there," she said.

"When?"

"When you were talking about marriage. I knew you were trying to get closer to Bierta, to catch her off guard."

He smiled. "Yeah, that's what I was doing."

"On the other hand," she continued, linking her hands around his waist, "'a promise made is a debt unpaid.' I heard that somewhere."

"It's from a Robert Service poem," Pierce said, his voice as soft as the night. "It's called 'The Cremation of Sam McGee.' The line goes, 'Now a promise made is a debt unpaid, and the trail has its own stern code.'"

"Well, so does this princess," she murmured, gazing up at him. "A verbal contract is binding in my country."

He leaned down and kissed her nose. "Mine, too," he said.

"And so I expect a modest but sparkling diamond on my ring finger by the end of the year and a baby by, oh, let's say, a year so later—"

She didn't get another word in, but she didn't

mind. Kissing him was way more fun than talking ever could be, and when he swept her into his arms and claimed her lips, she knew she was kissing her future.

"Let's go home," he murmured at last.

And they did.

Epilogue

"You left your queen wide-open," Birch Westin said, chuckling. "You're letting me win, young lady, but I don't care." He lifted the ivory queen and set her aside. "Check."

Analise smiled at her father-in-law-to-be. He'd accepted Pierce's decision to stay on the ranch with tears in his eyes, forever endearing himself to her.

"I'm not letting you win," she said, absently scratching Bonnie's ears. "I'm just a little distracted."

"There they come," Birch said, looking up from the board.

She'd heard the hoof beats at the same time he did so she was already looking up as the three horses carrying three men thundered up the rise and into the huge yard.

The Westin brothers, one better-looking than

the next, all of them cut from what was intrinsically the same mold. Cody the oldest, the darkest of them with deep brown eyes and hair. Cody, quiet and taciturn and yet boiling inside with things he wouldn't or couldn't talk about. He'd turned up a few days after the police finally left the Open Sky, refusing to discuss where he'd been, anxious, he said, to get on with the real world, and that meant this ranch.

And he'd obviously been delighted his younger brother had finally come to his right mind and returned to Wyoming.

It had been Cody who managed to calm down the elder Garvey when he showed up demanding revenge for his boys. Pierce had been way too close to the death and destruction Lucas and Doyle had inflicted to be patient, but Cody had somehow managed it.

Adam was the youngest of the brothers and the shortest at six feet even. He waved at her from the saddle, his smile one of the better smiles in the world. His eyes were a silver-gray, his hair a shade or two lighter than Pierce's, his skin tanned to a honey color. He'd arrived back on the ranch before the police were through with their investigation, and his clear head and wry sense of humor had helped everyone through the trying days ahead.

He, too, had welcomed Pierce home with

enthusiasm, and he'd welcomed Analise into the family though the wedding was still a few months off.

After Pierce dismounted, he wrapped the pinto's reins around a hitching post, and walked toward them. Analise's breath caught in her throat at the look in his eyes and she wondered how she was going to bear being away from him for a month.

"You all packed and ready to go?" he asked, coming to a halt right in front of her.

"Jamie and Mike loaded everything in the truck for me."

"Great." He turned to his father. "We found the five escaped heifers over in the gulch, each with a new baby. Cody and Adam are going to go out and bring them in while I drive Analise to the airport."

"Good, good," Birch said. He got to his feet and using a cane, came around the small picnic table where they'd set up the board in order to take advantage of the afternoon sun. "You take care, young lady, and you come back soon."

She had risen to accept his hug. "I will. Thanks for everything."

He looked from her to Pierce and sniffed. "Damn pollen." With a nod, he turned and made his way toward the cabin where Pauline beckoned him.

Pierce put his arms around Analise's waist and pulled her close, gazing into her eyes. "Don't go back to Chatioux and remember how nice it is to be one of the idle rich, okay?"

She loved the way his eyes delved into hers. "I know where I belong," she whispered. "But I have to talk to my parents and Ricard in person. I have to see Toby and reassure him. I've put all this off too long as it is."

"I know you have. And in a month, as soon as calving season winds down, I'll catch a jet and come get you. I want to meet the in-laws."

"They're going to adore you," she said, leaning into him. "My mother is ecstatic that I fell in love with her old friend's son."

"So am I," he whispered and kissed her.

They broke apart at the sound of whistles and catcalls. Pierce's brothers grinned, then both tipping their hats at Analise and calling out farewells, turned and rode back the way they'd come.

"Where were we?" Pierce said.

She tipped his face down to hers, stood on tiptoe to kiss him. "Right about here," she said.

* * * * *

OPEN SKY RANCH *continues next month with* WESTIN LEGACY *by Alice Sharpe.*
Look for it wherever Harlequin Intrigue books are sold!

LARGER-PRINT BOOKS!
GET 2 FREE LARGER-PRINT NOVELS PLUS
2 FREE GIFTS!

Harlequin®

INTRIGUE®

BREATHTAKING ROMANTIC SUSPENSE